OCT 2 5 2015

W9-AKT-550

King and Queen

Tisha Raye

NO LONGER PROPERTY OF
SEATTLE PUBLIC LIBRARY

Life Changing Books

Published by Life Changing Books

P.O. Box 423

Brandywine, MD 20613

This novel is a work of fiction. Any references to real people, events, establishments, or locales are intended only to give the fiction a sense of reality and authenticity. Other names, characters, and incidents occurring in the work are either the product of the author's imagination or are used fictitiously, as are those fictionalized events and incidents that involve real persons. Any character that happens to share the name of a person who is an acquaintance of the author, past or present, is purely coincidental and is in no way intended to be an actual account involving that person.

Library of Congress Cataloging-in-Publication Data;

www.lifechangingbooks.net

13 Digit: 9781943174041

Copyright ©2015

All rights reserved, including the right to reproduce this book or portions thereof in any form whatsoever.

Follow us:

Twitter: www.twitter.com/lcbooks

Facebook: Life Changing Books/lcbooks

Instagram: Lcbooks

Pinterest: Life Changing Books

ON TO THE NEXT ONE

Bri

I sighed as I looked down at the time on my MacBook Pro. It was almost midnight. I saved the paper that I'd been working on for the past hour and shut the computer down. While I was busy typing my argumentative essay that was due for my English 111 class, Ty's lateness didn't bother me. Now that I was done, and I realized how late it was, I was pissed. He wasn't behaving like a man that wanted his girl back, but more like the dog-ass, hustler that he really was. A huge yawn was all the confirmation I needed to grab the keys to my cherry red Lexus ES, my crocodile embossed Alexander McQueen bag and head for the door. If Ty wasn't cheating, then he was making money and he spent way more time doing those things than being with me and I was fed up. I understood that if a woman didn't want a broke man she would have to deal with a busy man, but the same way he made time to cheat, he would have to find a way to make more time for me.

I froze in my tracks when the doorbell rang. I wondered who it could be and if I should even answer it. I bit my bottom lip and my heart pounded as I contemplated looking out of the peephole. It could have been one of Ty's side bitches or it could have been a jack boy. Being with Ty had me paranoid and I hated living like that but he was worth a whole lot of money and it made him and everybody close to him a target. Before I could make a decision, my cellphone rang. Looking down at the screen of my iPhone 6, I saw that it was Ty.

"Hello?"

"Hey bae. Chrome is on his way over there. Let him in. I'm right up the street. I know you're mad at me, but I swear I'm on the way."

I rolled my eyes and ended the call without even acknowledging what Ty had said. If he said he was up the street, that meant he was a good ten minutes away. I had been with Ty for three years, but we'd been broken up for three weeks. I left him plenty of times in the past for cheating, but his charming ass always found a way to lure me back. This time was different. This time, some pretty ass chick with a nice body was pregnant by him. Yes, I was pretty too, and my body was ok, but a baby was something that I couldn't look past. Ty had done a lot of damage to my heart over the years, but this was the one thing that snatched the shit from my chest.

I left Ty and went and stayed in a hotel room until I could figure out what to do. However, a week after leaving him, I found out that I too was pregnant. I reluctantly told him, but I made it clear that we weren't getting back together. Ty clearly didn't believe me because every day he was sending me flowers, or edible arrangements, cards, bears, balloons. I had finally agreed to come over and speak with him but I had no intentions of taking him back. He was a crazy ass nigga born in Haiti and moved to Miami when he was ten. He was hustling by 16 and had relocated to Raleigh, NC by the age of twenty-one and damn near took over the small country town. His light skin, wild locks that hung past his shoulders, ever present charm and swag to die for made him a hit with the ladies.

I went over to the door just as the bell rang again, and opened it for Ty's right hand man, Chrome. "What up Bri? That nigga ain't made it here yet?" Chrome asked.

"No. He said he was right up the street though."

Before Chrome could get all the way in the house, I saw the headlights of Ty's black Audi A8 L pulling into the driveway. I left the door cracked and went and took a seat on the plush, chocolate suede sectional. *Him and Chrome had better be done in fifteen minutes or my ass was leaving,* I said to myself.

Ty entered the house smiling, holding a dozen roses. He'd sent so many flowers over the last few days, my hotel room looked like a florists. I couldn't help but raise my eyebrow at his sexy bowlegged ass in his denim Diesel Safado jeans, a black tee and black Balenciaga sneakers. He walked over to me and kissed me on the lips.

"I'm sorry 'bout that love. Give me ten minutes and I'm all yours."

I took the flowers without speaking. I refused to show any weakness for Ty. He turned his attention to Chrome, giving him dap and signaling with a head nod to follow him into the kitchen.

When Ty spoke business or over the phone, he spoke in French or Creole. I had been around him so long that I understood some things, and even though I was scrolling through my phone looking on Instagram, I recognized the words, *nouveau, se connecter,* and *moins cher.* He'd basically just told Chrome that he had a new connect that was cheaper. The sudden urge to urinate hit me, and as I stood up to head to the bathroom, I heard something that sounded like a cannon. My heart thudded in my chest, as I heard several more sounds that sounded like multiple fireworks being let off.

I screamed and took off for the stairs, when a stinging, searing pain ripped through my left shoulder. Before I could make it to the first step, my head was yanked back forcefully by my thick, shoulder length, honey blonde dyed hair. Something hard poked me in the side and a gruff voice said, "Where the fuck is the money at?"

This couldn't be happening. My worst fear had come true. *Where were Ty and Chrome? Why was he asking me about the money?* Fear consumed me, and the intense pain from my shoulder along with the super tight grip he had on my hair kept me from responding and my captor didn't like that. He punched me in the head so hard, I got dizzy and stars danced before my eyes.

"You think this shit a game bitch?" he barked.

Tears rolled down my plump, golden colored cheeks and dripped off my chin. "Upstairs." Two figures dressed in black, with ski masked covered faces, raced up the stairs. The person holding the gun in my side nudged me. "Let's go."

My arm was becoming numb, but I did as I was told. We made our way up the stairs and to the master bedroom. The two guys that had gone up before us were already ransacking the room. I went straight to the closet, fearing that Ty wasn't present because he was dead. I opened the closet door and made my way inside. The closet was big enough for a couch to fit inside and still have room to move around in. It was filled with clothes, shoes and fitted caps. I went over to the safe that was hidden behind shoeboxes stacked on top of each other. I used my good arm to move the shoeboxes so that I could get to the safe. My hands were trembling, which made opening the safe difficult.

"Hurry up!" the masked man, pushed the gun deeper into my side. I got the safe open and was shocked to see one lone stack of money inside, along with one brick of cocaine, and Ty's platinum chain with a black, diamond encrusted crucifix on it. I knew that Ty never kept all his money in one spot, but there was often more than that in the crib.

"The fuck?" the gruff voice was clearly disappointed.

"Where the rest of the money at?"

"I don't know." I cried. Wrong answer. The asshole took his fist and punched me in the face; so hard I flew to the side and tripped over the shoeboxes. Once I was on the floor, he proceeded to kick me and punch me as I curled into a fetal position and cried. Ty had to be dead or this wouldn't be happening. After a good minute, my attacker grabbed the contents of the safe and fled the closet, stepping on my finger in the process. I lay there crying for a good minute, the pain was antagonizing. Breathing was even excruciating. When I realized that I was lying in blood, my survival instincts kicked in and I peeled myself up off the floor.

"Ugggg." I groaned. The pain was unbearable. I limped through the bedroom and slowly descended the stairs. Once I reached the last step, I entered the living room and grabbed my phone from the couch. I dialed 911 as my eyes darted around the room. Feathers from the couch were everywhere, two lamps were broken in huge pieces on the floor, and bullet holes riddled the wall. I sobbed as I went into the kitchen and almost threw up at the sight of Chrome sprawled on the floor with half his face gone, clutching a 9mm in his left hand.

"911, what's the address of your emergency?"

"313 Arbor Towne Drive. I've been shot." I cried as I scanned the huge kitchen looking for Ty's body, and to my relief didn't find one.

"Help is on the way, ma'am. Do you know who shot you?"

I became lightheaded and had to grip the marble counter top in front of me. "No." I said in a voice that was barely audible, and then I blacked out.

For the next twenty-four hours, I was in and out of consciousness. I had a broken rib, a fractured finger, took a shot in the shoulder and I miscarried. Each time that I woke up, there was a different person by my side, be it my grandmother, my best friend Syria, or my sister Jen. The one person that was never there was Ty. I had been asleep when police came to question me, but Syria had confirmed that Ty's body hadn't been found. *So where was he? Was he being held for ransom? If he was able to make it out of the house, why didn't he come back for me? Had they murdered him and taken his body somewhere?* There were too many questions and absolutely no answers. I was in no condition to stress or worry, but I couldn't help it. Something about this situation wasn't right.

FLASHBACKS

Pro

"I made breakfast for you baby." A sweet voice woke me up from my sleep. I opened my eyes and was damn near blinded by the bright sunlight, streaming through my large bay windows. I squinted my eyes and fixed my gaze on my girlfriend Mesha. She was standing directly in the sunlight and the rays from the sun made her appear as if she was glowing. Her peanut butter skin was make-up free and perfect, and her shoulder length, black hair was pulled up in a bun. The square framed Versace eyeglasses that she wore made her look innocent and she had the brightest smile on her face.

Mesha was holding a wooden breakfast tray, and on the tray was a white, square plate adorned with scrambled, cheese eggs, bacon, waffles, and strawberries. Beside the plate was a wine glass, containing a mimosa. I sat up in bed, prepared to take the tray from her, when the glass from the bay windows shattered. Mesha began screaming, and the tray slipped from her fingers, causing it to crash to the floor. Our food and beverages scattered across the plush white carpet, as Mesha continued with her ear piercing screams. I attempted to reach for her and out of nowhere, a small bullet hole appeared in the center of her forehead.

"Mesha!" I screamed out, but my voice couldn't be heard over her screams. I tried desperately to reach her, but just like that, she was gone.

I sat up in bed with my heart pounding in my ears. I looked frantically around my spacious bedroom, and realized that I'd been dreaming. I picked up the king sized pillow that lay beside me and threw it across the room. "Fuck!"

It had been four months since Mesha was murdered and every time I thought that the grief was getting a little easier to deal with and the guilt was fading a little, I would have another stupid ass nightmare, to make me relive that pain. I removed the red sheets and black comforter from my legs, and placed my feet on the floor. I picked up my lighter and a ready rolled blunt of Kush from my nightstand. I set fire to the blunt and took a long deep pull. As the potent weed sailed through my body, I painfully thought back to the night that I lost my soul…

I raced home at midnight, knowing that Mesh was going to be super hot with me. We were supposed to go to the movies four hours ago to see the new

Kevin Hart movie "Get Hard". I had every intention on being home by seven, but for some reason my phone was ringing three times as much that day, and I definitely wasn't complaining. I mostly sold weed, but I also dabbled in dog food, better known as heroin. My phone was ringing so much that I had to re-up twice that day. It was pay day for one of my white customers that despite being a heroin addict, he held a job. He turned two of his co-workers on to me and the three of them combined spent $400.00. There was no way that I could miss that money. Little did Mesha know, we desperately needed it.

Mesha was a good girl. I was the second guy she'd ever dated. Her first boyfriend was the nerdy type. Mesha was green to the game and not street at all, and yet she liked me. She was in college to be a nurse and she didn't do drugs, or party. We had pretty much nothing in common but that girl loved me to death. However, her parents hated me. They hated me so much that when Mesha refused to leave me after I caught a weed charge, her father cut her off financially, hoping that would make her leave me. It actually did the opposite, and she moved in with me and I became her provider.

I paid all the bills in our small, two-bedroom house in a decent neighborhood, and we shared my 5-series black Beamer. I never let Mesha know that it was taking all I had to provide for us. Sometimes I would give her my last to get her hair done, or buy an outfit. Thank God, she was ok with Bebe and other cheaper labels because I couldn't afford Prada and Gucci, but all of that was about to change. I was headed home with $9,500 in my pocket. Another day like that and I'd be able to buy Mesha a car of *her own. That would surely make her see that I could provide for her just as good as her father.*

I practiced my apology over and over in my head as I pulled up in the driveway. Mesha had called me three times and I had ignored each call. Shorty was prolly mad as hell, waiting on me at the door. I turned off my engine and exited my vehicle. Mesha wasn't really the nagging type and wasn't very confrontational, so I would let her get her anger out and then apologize profusely. I ran up the four porch steps, and opened the screen door. As I put my key in the hole, an eerie aura filled the air and it was more than a pissed off girlfriend. The hairs on the back of my neck stood up and I pulled my glock 45 from the waistband of my vintage Levi jeans.

As soon as I opened the front door, my heart plummeted into my stomach. Red footprints decorated the carpet, pictures that were once hanging on the walls, littered the floor, and the screen of my 62-inch television was shattered.

"Mesha!" I called out as I raced through the small living room and down the short hallway.

"No." I whispered as I entered my bedroom and found my mattress over turned and dresser drawers hanging out of their spaces.

The closet door was open and I knew that the pound of weed and $2,500 that was in there was gone. A stench assaulted my nostrils and I went further into the room. Sticking out from under the mattress were a pair of dainty, small, brown feet.

"Mesha, no." I moaned as I walked over to her and moved the mattress.

There lay my precious baby, wearing a white tee shirt drenched in blood. She lay there stiff and lifeless with her brown eyes open and a bullet in the center of her forehead, shooting her in the chest wasn't enough. I dropped to my knees and cradled her cold body. I rocked her back and forth as tears fell from my eyes onto her face.

"Baby please wake up. Baby please I'm sorry. God no, don't do this to me." I cried like a baby.

If this were a fairy tale, my tears would have awakened her. But this was real life and nothing could bring her back. Guilt rocked my soul as I thought back to the three times she called and I assumed she was calling to beef with me. If I wasn't a low-life ass drug dealer we would have been at the movies and she would have never been in danger. Her parents were right, she should have never been with a guy like me. She was too good for the grimy life that I had subjected her to. I mourned for a good five minutes before reluctantly letting her go. I gently lay her head on the carpet and called 911.

After that night, I took a few of my belongings and moved into a hotel. I couldn't get over the fact that my girl had died behind some weed and a few funky ass dollars. I was damn near comatose for three days. I couldn't eat or sleep, all I did was smoke weed and hate myself. I was a coward. I couldn't face her parents. It was my fault she was dead and we all knew it. I went to her funeral with no plans to go inside. I waited in the cut and after the service, I followed everyone to the burial site.

Tisha Raye

I waited patiently for everyone to leave after Mesha had been lowered into her final resting place. I then made my way over and looked down into the deep hole. I eyed the silver coffin and broke down once again.

"I'm so fucking sorry."

I hoped everyone was ready, because as soon as I found out who did that shit, the city of Raleigh was going to be painted in blood.

Once the blunt was gone, I snapped out of my fog and headed to the shower in my master bedroom. I lived in a hotel for two months, hustling and keeping my ear to the streets. I didn't like sleep, because sleep brought nightmares. I felt like I had a lead role in the movie *Nightmare on Elm Street*. I hustled like my life depended on it, and gambled on occasions. After two months, I moved into a three-bedroom, three-bathroom house in a gated community on the outskirts of Raleigh. I had a top of the line alarm system. What I should have had when I was living with Mesha.

I took a hot shower, and dressed in gray Polo sweats, a white Polo tee and red, white, and gray Bo Jacksons. I stuffed my MCM backpack with a pound of weed and twenty bundles of heroin and prepared to head out for the day. I didn't like riding with too much work in my possession. I didn't even have a trap spot, my phone rang so much that I trapped on wheels. I frequently got rentals, just to switch up cars, so my Beamer wouldn't be so hot.

I'd just locked my front door, when my cell phone rang. Looking down at the screen, I saw that it was my homie Jock. We'd known each other for about three years when Jock moved here from Cali and started copping weed from me. He sells coke, but his weed habit was so bad, that he copped ounces from me every four days, to personally smoke.

"What up?" I asked answering the phone.

"Aye homie, I got some information for you. It's what you've been waiting on, and I don't even want the money. I just don't speak over phones though, so meet me at Pullen Park at three."

I'd put word out that I had $1,000 for whoever could get me information on Mesha's murder. I was anxious as hell to find out what Jock knew. Looking at my black Movado watch, I saw that it was only ten am. Shit, three o'clock seemed like days away, but I had to respect Jock's gangsta.

"Aight fam, I'll be there." I ended the call and headed out to my car. Three o'clock couldn't come fast enough.

I served a few customers, and then headed to my mom's house around noon. I gave her money every Friday. Only one hundred dollars, I wanted to give her more, but Mesha's death freaked her out so bad that she wouldn't take any money from me, if she knew that it came from hustling. I had convinced her that I had a job painting houses, and various businesses. When she saw the house that I lived in, she was skeptical that I got money the legal way, but I told her that I made good money. That being said, I pretended that after I paid my bills, all I could afford to give her was one hundred dollars.

My mother was a housekeeper and she wouldn't even have to work if her husband wasn't a drunk. Growing up, my dad was a welder and with him and my mom's income, we lived in a nice two-bedroom home and they both had nice cars. My dad got hurt at work one day, and began trying to get workman's compensation. It took him over a year to get the settlement and in the time, my mom was the only one bringing in money and my dad had picked up a nasty drinking habit. My dad began drinking around noon and drank until bedtime. He was also a violent drunk that began putting his hands on my mother when he felt like it.

I was twelve and starting to feel myself, and a couple of times, I jumped in front of my father and dared him to touch my mother. He would laugh at me but he would also leave her alone for the moment. After a while, he just started hitting her when I wasn't there. Despite our strained relationship, when he got his large settlement, he gave me $800 to go shopping with and gave my mother a large amount of money. After paying the rent up for a year, getting some new furniture and catching up on the bills, he was almost broke again, but his monthly check was enough to cover the utilities, and other expenses. Once the bills for the house were paid, he would drink up the rest of the money.

He started cheating on my mom and staying out late and I don't even think she cared because when he wasn't home, she got peace. Once the year was up, and rent was due again, money started getting tight. Pretty soon, my dad's check would be gone and he'd be asking my mom for money so he could buy liquor. I gave my mom money so she could get gas, keep her hair done, or whatever she wanted. I made it clear to her that my money was not to get his ass drunk.

When I pulled up in the driveway, I saw that my mother was sweeping off the porch. I got out of the car and headed for the porch.

"What up ma?" I asked as I kissed her on the cheek. I get my light skin from my father. My mother is dark-skinned and I could tell from pictures, she was bad back in the day. She was still an attractive woman, she just looked tired and worn.

"Hey baby." my mother barely looked up at me, but I still noticed that her right eye was swollen. My body immediately tensed up and I clenched my fists. "That nigga ain't gone get enough of putting his hands on you is he?"

"Baby, I'm fine. You…"

I smacked my lips. "I don't want to hear that. How you fine and that nigga use you for a punching bag? Why do you always take up for him? You need to leave him!"

Before my mother could respond, my father pulled up in the driveway in his white Ford pick-up truck. My nostrils flared and panic crossed my mother's face.

She immediately stepped closer to me. "Prentice no."

I ignored her and stepped onto the porch step. My father got out of the truck and walked towards the porch looking from me to my mother curiously.

"Son?" he asked noticing my stance. I stepped off the porch and faced my father.

"What did I tell you about putting your hands on my mama?" I asked.

My dad laughed. "Little nigga, you might be taller than me, and you might be covered in tattoos, you might even run around in the streets like a common thug, but that's not what I raised you to be. You better back up out my face before you get hurt." He warned.

I wasn't phased. "Seeing as how you ain't shit but a drunk, you ain't raise me to be shit."

"Nigga…" before he could finish his sentence I rocked his ass. One right hook to the face, and my mother screamed as my father staggered. I took a step closer to him and he lost his balance trying to back up and fell. I towered over him.

"You beat my mom, but yo ass can't stay on your feet and go toe to toe with a lil nigga. Don't put your hands on her again." I stated as my father stared up at me. I went to my car and got in before I was tempted to finish his ass off.

I wasn't in the best mood after that, but I occupied my time by getting money. Before I knew it, it was 2:30. I headed to Pullen Park to meet Jock. I parked my car and sparked a blunt. My phone rang and I thought it might be Jock, but it was Stephanie. I sighed, I really wasn't in the mood to deal with her, but I answered. Stephanie was a female that I met last month at the club. I wasn't over Mesha by any means but I still had needs. I hadn't had sex in three months and I was horny. I made it clear to Stephanie that I didn't want a relationship and she was cool with it, or so I thought. I hit her three times total over a course of three weeks and then I fell back.

Since Mesha's death, I'd have times where I was ok and then there was times when I would shut everybody out. I didn't feel that I owed anyone any explanations, so when Stephanie called me going off about how she hadn't heard from me, I simply cut her off. "Yo."

"Hey Pro. I just wanted to let you know that…I'm pregnant." Her voice trailed off. I closed my eyes and silently cursed, remembering back to the night when the condom broke. I tried to remain calm.

"What you want to do?" I asked.

"I'm gonna keep it."

Wrong damn answer. "Shorty, you don't even work. My life crazy as hell right now and we not even together. You really want to bring a baby into this?"

"Yes I do." She replied adamantly.

I sighed, searching the parking lot for Jock.

"Stephanie I'm gonna hit you back." I ended the call without waiting for a reply. I looked at my phone and saw that it was three twenty. *Where the fuck was Jock?* My phone rang again and it was my best friend Wiz.

"Yo." I was becoming even more agitated.

"Nigga, you heard about Jock?" he asked.

My heart rate increased. "What happened?"

"Nigga spot got raided. He had like two hundred ecstasy pills and three pounds of weed. He under a 1.5 million dollar bond."

My eyes bulged out. "1.5 million for that? What the fuck them crackers trying to be funny?"

"I guess yo."

I threw my cell phone into my passenger seat. My day couldn't get any worse. I needed to know what Jock had to tell me about Mesha's killers!

THAT'S MY BEST FRIEND

Bri

I stayed in the hospital for four long days, and then I was released to the real world. It took a good three days for images of Chrome's body to stop plaguing my mind. I had called Ty's phone a good thirty times and it was going straight to voice mail. I was crushed, *where was he?* So many emotions were running through me, I felt that I was going crazy. I was mourning the child that I lost, shaken up from being so close to death, confused and worried as to where Ty was, and aggravated at the interrogation from police. The only thing that kept me sane I'm sure, was the medication that was constantly in my system. Between morphine, Lortabs, and Xanax, I was pretty much calm or asleep most of the time.

I was still sore and moving rather slow the day that I was released from the hospital. Jen showed up at noon looking like a pecan brown version of me. Jen was 5'6, with almond shaped eyes and a small beauty mark on her bottom lip. My sister was twenty-seven with five kids, but her body was out of this world. Her ass got fatter with each kid and her stomach was flat as a board. Jen sauntered into my room wearing a pair of black leggings, a red tight, V-neck shirt and a denim biker jacket, on her feet were Chanel sneakers. Her long 22-inch weave was bone straight with a part in the middle.

"You ready?" she asked popping her gum.

Jen was a piece of work, I loved her but I didn't really like her. She was the hood rat type of chick that I didn't associate with by choice. She had her first child at fourteen and her second at sixteen. As soon as she turned eighteen, she got a place in the projects and that's where she has lived ever since. Jen and I can both do hair. I had the desire to open a high-end salon, while she was content doing hair out of her kitchen. Her rent was only $50 and that included utilities.

When you stepped in her crib, you could easily forget that you were in the projects. She had the brown shades replaced with blinds. There was a 60-inch television in the living room along with a red sectional. She had gorgeous plants and wall art and top of the line kitchen appliances. She kept a very neat and clean home, and she was just fine living in the middle of the hood. She had security bars placed in the windows, so she wasn't too worried about burglars.

One problem I had with Jen was that she felt that keeping her kids dressed in name brand clothes made her a good parent. She never went to a PTA meeting, but would stand in line for the new Jordan's. The oldest two kids were pretty much in charge of the younger ones while Jen did hair, slept or partied. Jen also ran through men like water. She had three different baby-daddies.

"Actually, I'm going home with Syria." I said.

Jen rolled her eyes. "I wish you would have told me that before I came up here. I should have known Ms. Bougie wasn't gon' want to stay in the projects."

"It has nothing to do with that. All of your rooms are full and Syria has more space. Plus as soon as I get a place, I won't have to stay with anyone."

"Where you gon' get money from? Your little boyfriend done jumped ship."

I wanted to slap the shit out of that bitch. She said that shit like she enjoyed the idea of Ty pulling a disappearing act. Jen was a jealous ass bitch. That's the main reason she didn't like Syria, jealousy. Syria's boyfriend Dez had her living in a condo on the north side of Raleigh and had even paid for Syria to get ass shots, when she used to strip. Of course, as soon as he paid for the ass shots he got super possessive and made her quit dancing.

"Don't worry about where I'm going to get money from." I snapped as Syria came in looking like Kim Kardashian with a tan. She was wearing black True Religion jeans, a red True Religion hoodie and Ugg boots. Her long, jet-black weave was curled to perfection.

"Hey boo you ready?" she immediately grabbed my bags, ignoring Jen. Jen rolled her eyes once again and pouted like a little kid.

"I'm gone." She left the room.

"Bye." Syria called out in an effort to get under Jen's skin.

I pretty much rested the whole day, and the following day, I got Syria to take me to Ty's house. I had once again called his cell numerous times with no answer. My chest became tight as we pulled up in front of the house and I grabbed my .22 from my purse. Ty's car was still in the driveway.

"Where is he?" I mumbled as tears filled my eyes. Syria reached over and rubbed my back. I took a deep breath and opened the car door. Syria followed suit.

Once we entered the house, we saw that it was still in shambles. Ty hadn't been there. I rushed up the steps, not wanting to be in the house any longer than I had to. Syria and I headed for Ty's bedroom and I got a few clothes and shoes that I had left at the house when I moved out. I took the plastic container off the top shelf of the closet that contained important papers, and got Ty's key for his safety deposit box at the bank. Once we left the house, I told Syria to take my things to her house and I got in Ty's car and headed to the bank.

Fifteen minutes later, I was placing $50,000 inside my Jessica Simpson purse. I didn't know where Ty was, but I needed this money. All I had in my bank account was $2,000. I went right up to a teller and informed her that I wanted to get a safety deposit box, and I did so after I deposited $5,000 into my bank account. I then placed $30,000 in the safety deposit box. I was going to take the other $15,000 with me and put in my personal safe.

My shoulder was starting to throb, but I knew the pain pills would put me out and I had more business to handle. I went to a relator and applied for an apartment. I gave them my W-2's from the previous year and told them that I did hair. With my A-1 credit and willingness to pay the rent for six months, it took me less than two hours to be approved for a two bedroom, three bath. I popped a pain pill on the way back to Syria's and by the time I reached the guest room to lay down I was out like a light.

The next day, I decided to go to Jen's and visit my nieces and nephews. Tia was fourteen, Tyquan was thirteen, Tyrie was

ten, Kia was three and Kayden was one. When I pulled up, Tia
and Tyquan were out front with their friends. Before I could even
get out of the car, I noticed Dez coming out of Jen's apartment.
My mouth dropped. Dez was Syria's man! *As far as I knew, Dez
sold coke, not weed or pills which Jen did both, so why was he at her crib?
Probably because she's a hoe*, a voice said in my head. I waited for
Dez to pull off in his black Tahoe and I got out of the car.

Tia and Tyquan both ran over to me. "Auntie!"

"Careful." I said as they slammed their little bodies into me.

"Oh we're sorry. Are you ok?" they wanted to know.

I forced a smile. "I'm fine guys. What is your mom doing?"

"Probably smoking. She told us to come outside cause she
had company."

My blood began to boil. I loved Syria like a sister, but Jen
was my sister, so why would she even put me in this
predicament? I went back to my car and pulled out two ten-dollar
bills.

"Here." I handed the kids the money and their eyes lit up.

"Thank you!"

I headed inside the apartment and found Jen walking out of
the bathroom dressed in a short, red silk robe.

"Why was Dez here and you in here half naked?" I asked
cutting right to the chase.

Jen was an excellent liar, but I knew her. Her eyes shifted to the wall behind me and I knew she was guilty.

"How could you?" I asked before she could answer the first question.

Jen became defensive. "Please, that's your friend not mine. That nigga fucking half the city, why can't I get a piece of the pie just cause that's your girl? You act like she your damn sister!" Jen rolled her neck.

I squinted my eyes and shook my head at her in disgust. "You a nasty ass hoe and dick gone be the death of you." I turned and walked away.

"Fuck you!" Jen called out pissed off. I got in my car, heated and glad the kids had migrated up the block. No matter how dirty that bitch was, I couldn't rat on my own sister.

"Damn." I said, thinking that Syria deserved so much better than Dez.

I went and picked out furniture to be delivered to my apartment in two days. I got a simple cream-colored living room set and a king-sized bed with a huge, suede gray headboard. Once again, my shoulder was starting to throb, and after I went to Target and picked up bedding and cleaning supplies, I popped a pain pill and headed back to Syria's. I thought about the baby that I would never get to hold and for the hundredth time, my mind wandered to Ty. I knew his parents, sister and brother were in Miami but I didn't know them. It was crazy how I spent all that time as his girl, even lived with him and didn't know whom to contact from his family in case of an emergency. I didn't want to think that Ty had left me for dead in that house, but what else was I supposed to think?

I pulled up at Syria's more than ready to lie down. As soon as I entered the condo, I heard yelling.

"Get the fuck off me!" I immediately saw Dez with his hand wrapped around Syria's neck. The tighter he squeezed, the more hoarse her words became. She clawed at his hands, in an effort to get him to release her. Dez did release her, but as soon as he did, he slapped her.

"Nah, you was bad enough to hit me, hit me again bitch!" he yelled.

"I fucking hate you!" she cried as he mushed her upside the head.

"Ya'll chill out, please!" I ran over to them as best I could with my injuries. I had broken up fights between them before. The first time they fought in my presence, we jumped his ass but two days later, she was back with him. Ty made me promise to stay out of their shit, because if Dez hit me, he'd kill em, he said, so I did as I was told.

"I'm sick of this bitch!" Dez huffed and left the apartment. I comforted Syria as she cried on my shoulder.

"Syria, I got an apartment. I'm moving in in two days. You can stay with me, you don't have to deal with this bullshit."

Syria lifted her head from my shoulder and sniffed. "I know. I'll think about it." She promised, but I had a feeling she was lying.

The day after I moved into my apartment, I went to see this dude named Joe about a job at his strip club. Joe was known around the way as Dez's cousin and he was also a big, black fat nigga, but he had paper out the ass, as they say. Many people suspected that he hustled, but not too many knew for sure. I was one that knew, because he used to be Ty's connect. This dude had a Bentley and a Land Rover and had a huge house out in Durham. I had Ty's $50,000 but not knowing who robbed him, I didn't want to let it be known that I was holding. I had thought about relocating to Miami and opening a salon. In order to do that, I needed major chips, so I could kill two birds with one stone. I could save the remainder of Ty's money to open the shop and I would strip to earn money for the moment, and to be able to get a place once I moved in Miami.

I didn't have the biggest ass or boobs, and I was quite shy, but I knew that Syria used to make damn good money stripping.

If I played my cards right, I could make enough money in one night to damn near cover one months' rent on a place. I told myself that I would strip for six months and once that was over, I would be a resident of Miami.

"Damn baby. Hell yeah you got a job, when can you start?" Joe asked admiring me as I turned around slowly in his office giving him a review. I was still pretty sore from the beating and bullet.

"Next week." I said hoping that with a little more rest, I'd be fine.

"Cool. Let me holla at you about something." Joe motioned for me to take a seat ad he reclined in his chair. "As you know, Ty and I did business. When he got jacked, he owed me $50,000 for some fronted work. I made it my business to know who had done it and I found out. These particular gentlemen also killed another person a few months ago and her nigga wants revenge. I got a plan for us to all link up in the name of revenge. We both can gain here." Joe informed me.

I bit my bottom lip. Something was off. I specifically heard Ty say he had a new cheaper connect. Maybe I had heard wrong. Or maybe Joe was lying. Maybe if I went along with the plan, I could find out what happened to Ty. The latter idea made my heart flutter as I thought of piecing together this puzzle. If Joe was on some other shit, I'd find out soon enough. I needed to know where Ty was.

"I'm down." I stated.

YOU GOT MY BACK?

Pro

"Where you at nigga?" Wiz asked me when I answered my phone.

"Headed to see one of my white boys, what up?" I asked pulling into traffic.

I was on the highway, headed to see one of my customers that was about to spend $100. It was only noon and I was almost out of heroin. I had a galaxy 5 as well as an old ass flip phone. I conducted business on the flip phone, and even still, I didn't discuss business over the phone. I didn't trust smart phones and new technology wasn't about to get me jammed up.

"Joe called me, the nigga want to meet with you. Why I don't know, but you know I'm down to go with you." Wiz informed me.

"Joe?" I questioned.

I went to Joe's club a few times a month and whenever we saw each other, we spoke, but we definitely didn't have dealings outside the club. I heard that Joe hustled, and I didn't doubt it, but that was that man's business. I tried to never concern myself too much with what the next man was doing. Even though we'd never had a negative run in, I was suspicious of Joe wanting to meet with me.

"Yeah Joe. I told him to give us an hour. If you not trying to go, just give me the word."

"Nah, I'll go. Let me handle this business right quick, and I'll come scoop you in about twenty minutes."

"Bet."

I was still heated about Jock getting knocked. His people was trying to get him a bond reduction, but I wasn't holding my breath. He had information that I desperately needed but there was really no way for him to relay it to me. Now Joe was requesting to meet with me. It was a little weird, but I was going to go with the flow. I served my customer and headed across town to meet Wiz. I drove a good 100 miles a day, trapping all over the city and my pockets were heavy because of it. I'd contemplated just selling weight, but real spill, you can make more if you bust your shit down and sell it however. Just because a person serves fiends or users and not dope boys doesn't mean he not getting paper, and my stash was proof of that.

It didn't take me long to get to Wiz. He lived on the North side of Raleigh in an apartment with his girl Amy and their one-year old daughter McKenzie. Amy was a CNA, and just like Mesha's parents hated me, her parents despised Wiz. I loved basketball in school and didn't really have friends, just associates to hoop with. Wiz didn't play ball, but we hit it off one day in in school suspension and we've been tight ever since. His father is addicted to crack, so many days we bonded over stories of how we hated our fathers. I had Wiz's back and he had mine.

Wiz came out to the car dressed in black Akoo jeans, a red Akoo shirt and a black leather jacket. Black Timberlands decorated his feet. It was the middle of January, but it wasn't freezing out. Wiz got in the car smoking a blunt, and I wondered if that was all he was high on. Wiz was a live wire that would shoot first and ask questions last. He did weed, molly, x, and every now and then coke. I wasn't into all that shit, weed was enough for me. And as far as busting my gun, I would definitely do it, but I was a little more strategic with my movements. Wiz and I balanced each other out and made a great team.

During the ten-minute ride to Joe's club, we smoked and made small talk. I filled Wiz in on Stephanie's pregnancy and he shared stories of his latest baby mama drama. Once we arrived at the club, I took my .45 from under my seat, and placed it in the waistband of my jeans. Wiz and I exited my vehicle and approached the club. Joe served food during the day, and usually drew an ok sized crowd. The soul food was good as hell; the menu had everything from chicken and macaroni and cheese to collard greens and shrimp. There were about seven cars sprinkled around the parking lot. Wiz and I entered the large club and was met by one of the bouncers, Bear.

Bear was even more fat, black and ugly than Joe. "What up? The boss is expecting you. Follow me." he instructed us and we did just that.

We climbed a flight of stairs and walked past the VIP booths into a small office. Joe was sitting at his desk talking on the phone. He looked up as we entered the room and held up his pointer finger, signaling to us that he'd be right with us. Sitting in a chair, directly in front of Joe's desk was a female. Lil mama was bad. She had honey colored skin, and long platinum blonde weave that stopped just above her ass. She was dressed in a pair of colorful, tribal print culottes pants and a matching crop top that stopped above her pierced belly button. On her feet were powder blue, pointy toe heels and she had large, diamond hoops in her ear. Her entire left arm was covered in a tattoo sleeve and she had almond shaped eyes. She looked classy as fuck, sprinkled with a touch of hood.

Wiz and I remained standing as Joe wrapped up his call. Once he was off the phone, he gave us his attention. "Gentlemen thank you for coming. Wiz I appreciate you giving your man the message. However, there is some very sensitive and personal information to be discussed here, so I respectfully ask that you wait for your man at the bar. Have a drink on me. I assure you that Pro is in good hands."

Wiz looked at me for confirmation to leave. It didn't matter if we were in Joe's office or his club, if I didn't want Wiz to leave he wasn't leaving. My curiosity was piqued however and I gave him a slight head nod, signaling that it was ok for him to bounce. He did so, with Bear following behind him. I was shocked that the female stayed behind. I moved over to the chair that was directly beside her and took a seat, anxious for Joe to get down to business.

"Pro this is Bri. Bri this is Pro." Joe paused as he lit a blunt and took a deep pull from it. He blew out the weed smoke and continued his conversation. "Pro, Bri used to go with one of my customers. Not a customer from the club, but another kind of customer if you catch my drift. Well, one night he was robbed and Bri was brutally beaten. The people that robbed Ty, took

$50,000 that belonged to me. I just recently found out that the people that robbed you and killed your girl are the same people that robbed Ty. I am aware that you have a reward out for this information. I don't want the money, however. Bri has agreed to work with you, to help set these fuck boys up. You get to vindicate your girls' murder and after you hit the niggas, we can spilt the take that's all I ask." Joe once again inhaled weed smoke into his lungs.

My blood automatically began to boil and my trigger finger began to itch. I had been waiting four months for this information. I was ready to get at those niggas today, fuck planning and waiting. I didn't want to come off as unappreciative of the information that Joe had given me though.

"So how is she going to help me?" I asked.

Before Joe could answer, he went into a coughing fit from the potent weed he was smoking. I patiently waited, as he sounded like he was coughing up a lung. Once he was done choking, he composed himself and continued.

"Simple. We can do this the John Wayne, shoot em up bang bang way, or we can be smart about this. Nobody wants to go to prison. The head nigga of the crew, Crim frequents my club. Bri is about to start dancing here. She can get you close to the nigga, if you just have a little patience and not go crazy. I understand you want the nigga in the dirt and that will happen in due time."

This nigga sounded like he was going to be calling the shots and I didn't like that, but I had to respect it. I took a deep breath. "So what's the plan?" I asked.

"You and Bri go out to the bar and get acquainted. Have some drinks on the house and eat some food. Talk." Joe stated.

His words felt like a dismissal, so I stood up and Bri followed suit. We headed to the bar, and sat on the barstools. A cute, dark-skinned thick bartender approached us right away, ready to take our orders.

Bri went straight for the jugular. "Let me get shrimp, fries and a bottle of Belair Rose champagne."

The bartender slash waitress scribbled on her pad and then turned to me. I wasn't hungry. "Double shot of Patron." I said.

Once the bartender walked away, I got down to business. "So what happened with your man?" I needed details. If I had to work with shorty and let her watch me do dirt, I had to trust her. Bri shifted on her stool like she was uncomfortable.

"One night I was at his crib. He came in and was talking to his friend. Next thing I know, niggas ran up in the spot shooting. I got hit in the shoulder and his boy Chrome was killed. One of the guys made me take him to the safe, but the only thing in it was $1,000 and Ty's chain with black diamonds in it. That pissed him off and he beat my ass. I ended up in the hospital and lost the baby I was pregnant with. Crazy thing is though, I assume Ty made it out the house. No body has been found, but he's MIA. I haven't heard from him."

I frowned up my face in confusion as our drinks were placed in front of us. "Come again."

"I don't know what happened or what to think, but Ty is nowhere to be found. Maybe they killed him and tossed the body. I have no idea."

I threw back the strong, alcohol and processed what shorty was saying. Dude made it out the house and was MIA. That didn't sound right. I decided to leave that part of the story alone for now. "So how we gone play the situation with Crim?"

"I'm gonna try to get him to take me out on a date. I'll then place a tracking device on his car, so that you can find out where he lives and hit him."

I nodded my head slowly. "That sounds like a plan. Let me get your number."

I pulled out my flip phone and took her number and then gave her mine. Bri's reaction to my flip phone let me know that she was a thorough chick that had dealt with a real street nigga. Most females frowned up their face at my phone, and automatically assumed I was a broke nigga, and those are the materialistic birdbrains that I don't give the time of day. Bri never even flinched at my phone. At that point, Wiz came over from playing pool.

"What's good fam?"

"I'll tell you in the car. Come on." I stood up. "I'll get at you Bri."

After I dropped Wiz off, I went back to trapping, but my mind was racing a mile a minute. I was happy to finally have the drop on these niggas, but I was also skeptical about doing dirt around or with a female and a female that I didn't know at that. The fact that her man was MIA was a little odd to me. But even with all of the uncertainties, I was glad to be one step closer to revenge. I had never put my hands on a female and to know that these punks made a habit of beating and killing women, made me want to put my murder game down strong. I smoke no less than five blunts a day, so I made my usual stop at the store for a box of cigars. As I headed into the store, I saw a nigga that I had seen at the strip club before, but couldn't place his name. He seemed to know me though.

"Pro, what up? Let me holla at you for a minute." The tall, dark-skinned guy said sniffing and pinching his nose. Maybe he had allergies, or just maybe he had a habit of sniffing shit up his nose. I approached him hesitantly.

"What's your name, bruh?" I asked.

"Dez. I copped some weed from you before. Aye, I just want to put it in your ear that I got this custom made chain with black diamonds in it. Nobody else ain't got no shit like this, ya feel me? That shit cost a grip, but I'm willing to come off of it for five bands." Dez looked around nervously.

I should have rocked that nigga. Bri's words came back to me. I remembered her saying her dude had been jacked for a chain with black diamonds in it. This fool was trying to sell me a chain that could possibly get me murked.

"Nah bruh I'm good." I said heading into the store and not waiting for a response. This encounter only caused my mind to be plagued with more questions. *How did Dez end up with the chain? Was he one of Crim's flunkies? Did he have a hand in killing Mesha?* It took everything in me not to go back out of the store and hem Dez up and ask him those questions but I played it cool. In due time, I would know what was up.

My cell phone rang, and I saw an unfamiliar Atlanta number. "Yo." I barked into the phone.

"What up Pro? This Jock. Nigga, I know yo ass probably been like what the fuck? I got my people to call you on three way. I got a bond reduction, but I still got to put up collateral. One of my bitches in Virginia is gon' put up her house. I should be out this bitch in no more than two days. As soon as I touch down, I'm gon' hit you. Just be easy out there playboy and watch *everybody,* you feel me?" he asked emphasizing the word everybody.

"No doubt bruh, soon as you get out, get at me."

"Aight, one."

I ended the call and sighed in frustration. I needed to know what information Jock had because at this point, some shiesty shit was going on and I needed to find out what. I had the feeling a lot of blood was about to be shed, but as long as it wasn't mine, I was good.

MAKE THAT MONEY

Bri

I gave myself a once over in my full-length mirror. Dressed in a knee-length denim skirt, a denim blouse tied at the waist, and thigh-high Tom Ford boots, I was headed out on a date with Crim. I silently scolded myself as I placed my blonde tracks up into a messy bun on top of my head.

"You're crazy as hell to be going out with this psychopath." I sighed and placed diamond studs into my ear. Ty was still gone and my heart was still aching. I couldn't see a baby without being sad, or see a couple without grieving my relationship. I didn't want him dead but for the way that he had abandoned me, he better be.

I reached into my Chanel purse and took out a prescription pill bottle. The only way that I could make it through this date without freaking out would be to pop a half a Xanax. A whole one would put me to sleep. I placed the pill on my tongue and washed it down with bottled Fiji water. I then added nude Mac gloss to my lips and placed Tom Ford shades over my eyes. I reminded myself for the tenth time that I was doing this for a good reason.

My first night at the club, Joe had pointed Crim out to me and I approached him and flirted a little. He'd made twenties rain on me during my stage dance, before I even knew who he was. I almost blew my cover, when he asked for my number. I hesitated and he said, "Ma you think this a game? I want your sexy ass." It was his voice from that night. He was the one that had attacked me. Tears filled my eyes and I couldn't breathe. I was two seconds from running away, until I remembered the baby that I lost. I composed myself and gave the bastard my phone number.

My first night dancing I made $745.00, which wasn't bad at all. I couldn't even enjoy it, because I went home and cried. My life up to the night that I was beaten was fine and now it was a mess. Some days, I just wanted to curl up in a ball and die, but most days I made myself shake that shit off. I still wasn't speaking to Jen's grimy ass and aside from my grandmother and Syria, I had no one.

Me and Jen's dad was murdered when I was four. He got into an argument with a man over a woman and was shot in the back. Three years later, my mother hooked up with a man named Eddie. He was ok, until he and my mom argued and he would beat her like she was a man. This went on for ten years and they had the most dysfunctional relationship I had ever seen. You would have thought that my mom would have left him for beating on her, but one night she caught him cheating and begged him not to leave her. When he told her that the relationship was over, she shot him six times. She's now serving a thirteen-year prison sentence. I write her at least once a month and visit her two or three times a year. Deep down, I was bitter that she chose a man over her kids and her freedom.

There was no way I was letting Crim know where I lived, so I had agreed to meet him at the restaurant. I tend to overthink things so on the drive to Bonefish Grill, I was worried that someone would see me and question how I was already out with the next man when Ty had just recently…disappeared. Raleigh was a pretty big city, but as in every city, certain people have "hood fame" and Ty was definitely a hood star. Since he was so popular, guess who else was? I didn't care for the spotlight, but some chicks, like Jen live for that shit. I didn't enjoy walking in a club and half the people there knew who I was just on the strength of my man. People love to talk and if I was spotted with Crim, which would surely make the hood news.

As I was pulling into the parking lot of the restaurant, my Xanax started to kick in. It didn't completely calm me down but I was much less anxious and apprehensive as before. I spotted Crim's white C-class Benz and parked two cars over. I checked my bag and made sure that the tracking device was inside. I exited the car, and saw Crim leaning against his vehicle staring at me lustfully. I felt the urge to vomit. Surely he had to know who I was and that made me nervous as hell, and the fact that he had assaulted me and could seem so relaxed in my presence was disturbing.

Crim stood up straight as I approached him and twirled a toothpick in his mouth, never taking his eyes off of me. He was dressed in black Levi's, a red Marc Jacobs sweatshirt and red and white Louboutin sneakers. Crim wasn't fat, but even through his sweatshirt, I could see the bulge of his belly. He ate good often and exercised never. He had dark skin and a baldhead, with a beard gave him a Rick Ross type appeal. I spotted the Rolex on his left wrist and assumed that he made pretty good money as a low life jack boy.

"Hey beautiful." He smiled as I approached. A lump formed in my throat and my knees buckled, how was I going to pull this off? I gave him a tight smile as he hugged me and my body tensed up. It took everything in me not to take off running. "You ready to eat?" he asked oblivious to my discomfort.

"Yeah. Oh wait, shit, I forgot to tell my sister something. Go ahead and get the table, I left my phone in the car." I dug through my bag, pretending to be looking for my phone.

"You want me to wait?" he asked in that irritating ass gruff voice.

"Nah I'm starving. If you can go ahead and get seated and order me a sweet tea, that'd be good."

"You got it baby." Crim walked off and I headed back to my car with tears in my eyes.

"Man up bitch, you can do this." I gave myself a pep talk as I unlocked my car and opened the door. I leaned into the car and pretended to be searching for something. I grabbed an ink pen and closed and locked my door. When I got by Crim's car, I dropped the pen on the ground. I pretended to be looking for it as I walked around the car. I quickly squatted down and placed the tracking device under the car. I then stood up, wiped the lone tear off my cheek that had fallen from my eye, and headed inside.

I found Crim seated in the back. The waiter was placing the drinks on the table. I sat down and we ordered our food. Once the young, white, flamboyant male waiter walked away, Crim clasped his hands together and adjusted himself in his chair.

"So I take it you single? I guess I should have asked that at the club huh?" he smirked.

I stared at him for a second and fought the urge to jump across the table and claw his eyes out, but knowing that he would soon be worm food comforted me. "I been single for a minute. Me and my ex were contemplating working things out, but that didn't happen." I grabbed my phone and looked at it to see that Pro had texted me a few minutes earlier and made me aware that he was outside if I needed him. I read the message more than once, anything to avoid looking into Crim's face.

"What happened?" he asked.

I looked up at him with a dead serious face. "Stuff."

Crim held his hands up in mock surrender. "My bad baby. I know break-ups can be nasty."

I spoke before he barely finished the sentence. I didn't want to keep listening to the bullshit that he was spitting. "What about you? You got a girl or a wife?"

Crim removed the toothpick from his mouth. "I been dealing with my kid's mom for thirteen years. We go through our shit, but she ain't going anywhere. I still do me." he said arrogantly.

"I'm sure." I threw him a fake smile. I wanted this date to be over with ASAP. This nigga was making my skin crawl. Crim made small talk throughout the meal and I must say, I think I did a good job of pretending that I was enjoying myself. Once we were done eating, he asked when we would be able to chill. I wanted Crim to pay for what he had done, but I wasn't willing to sleep with him to do so and I was apprehensive about being alone with him. I wasn't interested in going to his place, so we agreed that soon we'd chill at the room. Hopefully, Pro would have killed him by then and the fat bastard would be a distant memory.

When I got back home, I found Syria getting dressed. She'd been staying with me for three days. Dez had jumped on her and choked her until she pissed on herself and passed out. He'd always dabbled in coke, but lately according to Syria, he was doing it more and it made him violent. He had been blowing her up and I was glad that he didn't know where I stayed, no one did, not even my sister. I was glad that she had left, but knowing her, she'd go back soon, especially when her money started getting low.

"Where you headed to?" I asked her admiring how cute she looked in her pink jeans, white and pink floral print blouse tied at the waist and white Versace flip-flops. She added gold bangles to her left arm.

"Out with Rico." She gave me a sneaky grin.

My eyes bugged out. "Rico who? I know not Rico with the Hummer."

"Yep, that Rico." Syria flipped her long Malaysian hair over her shoulder.

"Um, you mean the Rico that Dez doesn't like? The one that Dez fought in the club last year?" I asked not believing she was about to play this game.

"Yep that Rico." She repeated. "I saw him at the mall and that nigga is fine. Me and Dez are done for good this time and I mean it. Why can't I date who I want?" she asked like she really needed an answer to that dumb ass question.

"Maybe because you just left him three days ago and the nigga going crazy trying to get you back. Syria don't do this, I don't have a good feeling about it."

Syria grabbed her white Chanel bag and gave me a comforting smile. "Don't worry boo I got this. It'll be ok, we just going to dinner and a movie. I'll be back in a few hours." Syria rubbed my arm and headed out the door.

I stared after her. "Lord please watch over her." I mumbled.

Crim came to the club that night after I had been at work for about three hours. I'd already made $680.00 and I still had two more hours to go. On a slow night, I might only leave with three of four hundred but on a good night, I could take home $1,200 easy. Crim grabbed my arm as I walked by him.

"What up sexy? I got a room not far from here at the Marriott, you down to chill with a nigga?" he looked me up and down and licked his thick lips.

"No doubt. I'll follow you from here when I get off." I said in a sweet voice. The blunt of Kush I'd smoked along with the three shots of vodka I had downed made him more tolerable than previously.

"Aight sexy." He smiled and smacked me lightly on the ass. I couldn't control the nasty look I shot him, that didn't match the pleasant demeanor I had just displayed. I hurriedly walked off and went to the back to text Pro. He messaged right back telling me that he was on the way and would be outside in a brown Caprice. I put my phone and money away and headed back out to get that money.

Once the club closed, I headed to the back and got dressed in gray Bebe velour sweats and a white tank top. I slid into a matching gray Bebe jacket and placed white Nike's on my feet. I grabbed my bag and was escorted out of the club by Bear. There weren't many cars left in the parking lot and I spotted Crim sitting in his car immediately. When he spotted me, he started his car up and cut on his headlights. I scanned the parking lot and spotted the brown Caprice in the cut. I got into my car and started the ignition. Once Crim eased out of his parking space, I put my car into drive and did the same.

I looked into my rearview mirror and noticed Pro still sitting in the same spot. Crim and I pulled out onto the highway. I looked in the rearview mirror once again and saw Pro slowly creeping out of the parking space. I kept a close distance behind Crim initially, and then when we were about two miles from the club, I eased up off the gas. Pro sped up and pulled up beside me. He then passed me and cut in front of me so that he was behind Crim. Crim made a slight left onto the exit ramp, and Pro did the same. I kept going, headed for home. I hoped Pro would handle that nigga once and for all.

PAYBACK TIME

Pro

As soon as Crim got on the exit ramp, I rammed into the back of his car. It was the oldest trick in the book, but I was sure that he'd fall for it. Sure enough, as soon as I had tapped the rear of his Benz, Crim hopped out of the car looking pissed. My gun was already in my lap, as was Wiz's. Crim walked to the back of his car and surveyed the damage. I gripped my gun, as Crim looked angrily at the Caprice I was driving, ready for a confrontation. Or so he thought.

"Fuck wrong with you yo?" he barked angrily.

Wiz and I exited the car simultaneously with our guns drawn. At the sight of two guns on him, Crim's whole demeanor changed. His eyes widened with fear and he held his hands up. His eyes darted nervously from me to Wiz.

"Yo, my bad yo." he said, not even knowing what the fuck he was apologizing for.

I walked up on him because I wanted him to see my face and upon recognition, he looked as if he'd seen a ghost. I knew right then and there that he played a part in running up in my crib. Anger consumed me as I hit Crim in the mouth with the butt of my pistol. Blood immediately stained his teeth.

"Run your pockets bitch." Wiz stated.

There weren't any cars on the road, but I didn't want to chance anyone riding by, especially the police. Crim removed two wads of money from his pocket and no sooner than he did, I sent six shots into his body. He jerked back and forth with each shot, as if his body was doing a little dance. Crim finally hit the ground looking like Swiss cheese. I snatched the money from his hands, while Wiz ran to the car and went through it. I put one last bullet into Chrome's skull and then rushed back to the car. I waited anxiously for Wiz to get in and then I peeled off.

Wiz and I went to Crim's home, twenty minutes away from where we'd killed him. When it was all said and done, combined with what we got off him and out of his house, we had $35,000. Wiz and I were going to split that. I always tried to be a man of my word. I know that I initially agreed with Joe to spilt the take with him, but to split $35,000 three ways wouldn't leave Wiz and I with enough to accommodate us for the work we put in. We were the ones doing the robbing and the killing while Joe sat behind his desk and called the shots. He would never know what we got out of Crim's crib.

I headed to Bri's house. I was going to give her $10,000 of my share. I was sure that she'd agree to keep it on the hush from Joe. I tend to be a good judge of character and she seemed more 100 to me than Joe. It was just something about that nigga that I couldn't quite put my finger on. I texted Bri to let her know that I was ten minutes away from her crib. Wiz was once again beefing with Amy, so I dropped him off at my spot.

I knocked on Bri's door, carrying her share in my MCM backpack. It took her about ten seconds to answer. She came to the door in black boy shorts and a red sports bra. Her hair was pulled back in a ponytail and her face was make-up free. She was no doubt sexy to me. She could pass for being twenty, but she had told me she was twenty-nine and I was shocked. I was twenty-five and she looked better than a lot of chicks my age. It was damn near four in the morning when I stepped inside Bri's lavishly decorated home.

"I know it's late so I won't keep you. I got something for you though. We hit that nigga and he's no longer breathing." I informed Bri. She closed her eyes and a look of relief crossed her face.

"I never thought I'd feel so much joy from someone being dead." She shook her head as if she couldn't believe her own behavior.

"What that nigga did to you was foul shorty. What he did to my girl was beyond foul. He deserves everything he got. I actually wish I could have tortured his ass." I stated regretfully.

Before I could say anything else, there was loud ass persistent banging on Bri's front door. I immediately grabbed my gun from the waistband of my jeans and eyed her. If shorty was trying to set me up, she would join Crim in the afterlife. She looked just as confused as me, she even looked a little scared. Bri went over to the door and looked out the peephole. She opened the door and a light-skinned female attempted to come inside but she was snatched back.

"Syria!" Bri yelled stepping out of her front door. Still gripping my gun, I walked over to the door and peered outside. The nigga Dez that tried to sell me the chain was beating the brakes off shorty. She was screaming and trying to get away from him. Bri was making her way over to help her friend when I spotted a shiny, chrome 9mm in Dez's hand. I grabbed Bri around the waist, stopping her from getting in the dispute. I hated to see shorty getting handled like that, but I wondered if it was smart to shoot it out with this nigga over something that wasn't my business.

Bri struggled to get away from me and I was just about to tell her to chill and let me go holla at the nigga when Dez raised his gun and aimed it at Syria.

"No!!!!!" Bri yelled as Syria attempted to run. Dez let off a shot and Syria fell. All I could hear was Bri screaming and then I heard another shot. Dez was standing over Syria and had shot her once more. I maintained my tight grip on Bri as she screamed and frantically tried to escape my grasp. Dez stared at Syria for a second then he hopped in his car and sped away. Only then did I let Bri go. She ran over to her friend and dropped to her knees. "Nooooo! Syria, no!"

I let out a deep breath and called 911. This shit was beyond fucked up. Bri held Syria and cried until the ambulance came, but shorty was dead. She was dead as soon as she hit the ground. Bri was still hysterical, so I talked to the police. I told them everything I saw without dropping Dez's name. That nigga was going to be served with street justice for the fuck shit that he did. Watching Syria's lifeless body I couldn't help but think of Mesha.

It was damn near seven in the morning by the time Bri's crib was clear. She'd cried so much she was hoarse. "Go hop in the shower bae. You got blood all over you." I said gently. Her eyes were damn near swollen shut from crying. I was exhausted but I couldn't leave her until I knew that she was good. I sat on her bed and waited for her to get out of the shower. I rolled a blunt as I waited.

I was halfway through the blunt when she emerged from the bathroom, wearing a white tank top and black leggings. She looked like she had no fight left in her. I couldn't help but to place my blunt in the ashtray on her nightstand and walk over to hug her. As soon as I wrapped my arms around her, she buried her face in my chest and cried. I held her tight as she cried for a good ten minutes. "You smoke?" I asked. She nodded and I retrieved the blunt from the ashtray and handed it to her. She sat down on her bed and began to smoke.

"You gon' be ok?" I asked. I was really worried about shorty, she'd been through a lot. She nodded. I didn't believe her. "You got something to help you sleep?" I asked. Once again she just nodded. She stood up and went to her purse. She then took out a prescription pill bottle. I got up and headed to her kitchen. I opened her fridge and removed a bottle of apple juice. I took it to her and shorty popped a Xanax into her mouth. I peeled back her covers and she climbed in the bed.

"Who was that?" I asked her.

"My best friend Syria. Dez was her boyfriend, but she left him a few days ago because he was beating on her. She left earlier saying she was going to dinner and a movie with someone and she'd be back. Where all this shit came from, I have no idea."

"How well do you know Dez?" I asked her.

"They been together for a minute. I never cared for him too much but that was her nigga so it was what it was. We wasn't friends or nothing."

"I saw the nigga at the store the other day and he told me that he had a rare, custom made chain for sale for five bands. He said the necklace had black diamonds in it."

Bri squinted her eyes. "What?"

I nodded my head. Bri's brows wrinkled in confusion. "That had to be Ty's chain, but Joe said the niggas that ran in Ty's crib were Crim, and his boys Zoe and Reggie. Maybe one of them gave Dez the chain?" she looked confused.

I shook my head. "Who knows, but I do know that nigga definitely got the necklace. Don't worry about that though. Get some sleep and call me if you need me, ok?"

Bri nodded and I reluctantly stood up hating to leave her. I exited her crib and shook my head. Loving a street nigga was definitely stressful and a lot of these chicks deserved so much better.

I went home, showered and crashed for about five hours. I then woke up and got dressed for the evening. I had a message from Joe to come to the club. I headed that way, this time without Wiz. I had already spoken to him before I went to sleep and told him that Crim didn't have shit in his crib. He didn't seem too concerned but maybe he didn't believe me and that was what the meeting was about. Oh well, I was ready for whatever.

Again, when I entered the club Bear led me to Joe's office. When we entered, Joe was rolling a blunt. "What up Pro?" he asked cheerfully.

"Nothing much, what's the business?" I wanted to get to the point. I sat down in the same chair that I had occupied the last time.

"I got Reggie's info. Nigga live in Greensboro, but he get money here. I got his address. He's in town now, but will be headed back to Greensboro the day after tomorrow. I think it will be best to get him in Greensboro." Greensboro was two hours away.

I nodded my head. "That's not a problem. What's that nigga's info?"

Joe gave me the necessary information and I left his office. I got a call from the same Atlanta number that I had spoken to Jock on. I answered quickly. "Hello?"

"What up my G, I'm home. Come to my cousin spot out in POA."

"Bet, I'm like five minutes from there."

I headed to the spot glad that I was going to finally get the info that Jock had for me. POA was a huge ass apartment complex on the south side. I pulled up in the parking lot and got out in such a rush I damn near forgot to lock my doors. I walked up to building 301 and went up to the third floor. After tapping on the door, Jock's cousin a dark-skinned gay nigga named Ken opened the door. "Hey, he right in here." Ken said as I followed him into the living room. I found Jock sitting on a brown leather couch. Upon seeing me, he stood up and gave me dap.

"What up my nigga? Shit been hectic. So look, cutting to the chase. The word that I got was that Joe put Crim and two of his niggas on you. He felt like you was starting to do it too big on the heroin tip but you wasn't copping from him."

I was so hot, I'm surprised that steam wasn't coming from my ears. This fuck ass nigga had set me up and in turn now had me gunning for the very niggas he put on me. He was a dirty son of a bitch. Feeling that I could trust Jock, I ran the situation down to him. He looked shocked in the end.

"That nigga think he smart. He got them niggas to rob you and now he using you to get rid of the niggas. That nigga foul. If you need me to help you ride on that nigga give me the word." Jock volunteered sincerely.

"Oh we gone definitely ride as soon as I finish killing his minions." This nigga had me fucked up.

I'M A DOWN ASS CHICK

Bri

I stared out of the passenger window of the white Charger that Pro had rented. It was three days after Syria's death, and Pro had told me that we could skip the Greensboro trip, but I told him I would go. I needed to get out of the house; I felt like I was suffocating. Every morning that I woke up, I prayed to God that it had all been a dream and that Syria was still alive. I knew that going out with Rico was a bad idea, but no matter how wrong she may have been, she didn't deserve to die for it.

It was four in the afternoon and the sun was shining bright. I looked up at the sky and wondered if Syria's soul was at peace. The clouds were so pretty and white, but life was so ugly and cold. It's crazy how the two mixed. I let out a deep breath. I had to get it together. In the past month, I had cried almost more than I had in my whole life. First Ty and now Syria. I was slowly losing everyone that I cared about. My life had gone from fun and care free to empty and dramatic. Even with the bullshit I had gone through with breaking up with Ty, I wasn't devastated or unhappy. I couldn't understand for the life of me how my life had become so turned upside down in the blink of an eye.

Pro passed me the blunt and turned the radio down. We had been riding for almost an hour in complete silence. "You good?" he asked sounding genuinely concerned.

I was anything but good, but yet I didn't say that. "Yeah, I'm ok."

My voice came out in a whisper. It was hard to lie under the circumstances. I appreciated how he had been there for me, but I didn't want to be a Debbie downer. I inhaled the weed smoked and wished like hell, it would take away the pain.

"How deep are you in with Joe?" Pro asked out of the blue.

I turned to look at him, wrinkling my brows in confusion. "What do you mean?"

"I mean how long have you known him, how close are y'all?"

"I don't really know him, I just know of him. Ty dealt with him on the business tip, but I had nothing to do with that. After everything went down with the robbery, I just knew I needed some quick cash so I could head to Miami in a few months and open a salon. Why what's up?"

Pro was silent, like he was hesitant to answer my question, or he just didn't want to. He finally took his eyes off the road and glanced over at me. I was beginning to wonder what the hell was up. I raised my eyebrows as if to say, ok spill the beans.

"Joe on some foul shit. I don't even know if I should be rocking with you, hell you could be in on it too. You a cool ass chick, I swear but Joe ass gone be in the dirt soon and I pray to God, I don't have to send you to join him." Pro looked dead ass serious. Fear and confusion gripped my body.

"Hold up, what the hell are you talking about?" I asked trying to grasp the concept that this dude had just low key threatened me.

"My people told me that Joe was the one that instructed Crim, Reggie and Zoe to hit me, and I'm willing to bet, he set up the shit with your man being robbed also. Nothing beats the cross but the double cross and this dirty ass nigga got me killing the very dudes he put on me. So it's only logical to look at you sideways. Maybe he wanted you to work with me so you can get close to me."

I turned my body as best I could seeing as how I was in a seatbelt. I wanted to be looking directly at this man because he was saying some crazy shit. "I'm not in on anything with Joe. He came to me with the information about those niggas robbing Ty. I knew something was off from the gate, because right before everything went down, I heard Ty say he had a new connect. However, Joe swears that Ty owed him for work, it just didn't make sense to me. Dirty ass nigga." I said the last part more to myself than Pro.

"And now that I think of it, Dez and Joe are cousins, and I know that was Ty's chain that Dez had without even having to see it." I felt the sudden urge to throw up.

"I'm not exactly sure what this cat is up to, but I may kill him before I even find out. I don't have time for games and this nigga tried me." Pro shot me another look that read he wouldn't hesitate to kill me if needed.

"I understand your apprehension, but I promise you, I don't deal with Joe like that. And if he played a part in what happened with me and Ty, and I'm actually working in this man's club…" my voice trailed off. This was like a ghetto version of Scooby Doo and I had no desire to look for clues and try to crack a case. It was entirely too much.

"Don't worry bout nothing. I got you." Pro said in such a soothing voice that I believed him. All a woman wanted was to feel protected and where Ty had failed, Pro was definitely picking up the slack.

We got a hotel room to chill in until Pro and Wiz decided to go stake out Reggie's crib. I was coming out of the bathroom when I heard Pro on the phone and he sounded upset.

"This some bullshit Wiz, how the fuck you gone flake on me? You should have just rode with me. Why is your girl always tripping? Fuck it yo, I can do this shit by myself." Pro angrily ended the call.

He had a look on his face that would have killed me if looks were able to accomplish that. I gathered that Wiz wasn't coming, and Pro was pissed. Actually pissed was an understatement.

"I'll go with you." I offered.

Pro looked up at me like I'd lost my mind. "Nah, I'm good shorty."

"I'm not saying I'm gone kill nobody, I don't want no parts of that, but you need an extra pair of eyes. I can wait in the car and be your lookout. Don't be stubborn." I said with my hand on my hip.

Pro's face softened. "I just don't want to put you in a dangerous situation, besides less participants, less witnesses."

"Look, like I said before I understand your concern but I am not a snitch. Being beaten bad enough to lose a child by someone that I never did anything to makes me want to see these niggas suffer. I am aware that there could be consequences. I'm not gonna fold under pressure and whether you want to admit it or not, you need an extra pair of eyes. Keep saying no and I'm gon' keep asking." I folded my arms across my chest and prepared to continue my argument if I needed to.

Pro stood up and went over to his Louis duffel bag and removed a .45 and handed it to me. I didn't like guns, but I kept that information to myself. Pro and I went and got some food from Zaxby's to kill time. We planned to go to Reggie's house around 10 pm. On our way over to Reggie's, the car was silent except for Yo Gotti blaring through the speakers. I was grateful for the silence. I was a ball of nerves and I didn't want Pro to catch on, not after I had begged to come along.

After ten minutes of driving, Pro pulled onto a dark residential street. He cut off his headlights and parked in front of a house that had a for rent sign in the yard. Pro pointed to a brick, two story house, three houses up from where we were.

"That's the nigga crib."

There was a white Dodge Magnum in the driveway, and one light on upstairs. "That's that nigga car. I'm going in." Pro said pulling his 9mm from under the driver's seat. He turned to look at me. "Just keep the car running, and sit here till I get back, cool?"

I nodded my head and licked my lips, which felt super dry. There was no turning back now. I tried to calm my nerves as Pro got out of the car. He pulled the hood from his black hoodie onto his head and walked up to the house. Once he reached the yard, he went around to the back of the house. I sat there anxiously chewing on my bottom lip for what seemed like forever, but in actuality had only been about seven minutes. I shifted anxiously in my seat, ready to see Pro walking on his way back to the car.

A few more minutes passed and I saw a red Altima cruising down the street. "No." I said as the Altima turned into Reggie's driveway. "Shit." I gripped the .45 Pro had given me in my hand. I strained my eyes to see who was in the car. A few seconds later, a female emerged from the car. It was too dark for me to get a good look at her, but I knew it was a woman.

I left the car running and hopped out of it. Her alone might not pose a threat to Pro but I couldn't let her get into the house. I broke out into a jog as she headed up to the porch. I certainly didn't want to kill her, but I didn't have anything over my face, so letting her see me was a no go. I crept up behind the woman, just as she was about to stick her key in the door and she must have sensed that someone was behind her, because she started to turn around. Before she could get a good look at my face, I hit her as hard as I could with the butt of the gun. She screamed and immediately grabbed her nose. I panicked and hit her again in the face, that time she dropped like a sack of potatoes. I jumped as a gunshot went off inside the house. There was too much damn noise, between her screams and that gunshot. Neighbors would surely hear the commotion.

I prayed that Pro had been the one to let off a shot as I hit the sobbing female once more for good measure, and that blow knocked her out. Before I could move, Pro ran from the back of the house carrying a white pillowcase. Our eyes met and he appeared shocked, but neither of us said a word. We took off for the car and once we reached it, we hopped in and he sped off.

"What the hell happened?" he asked.

"A chick pulled up in the driveway. I panicked, I didn't want her to go in the house and see you."

Pro turned to look at me and he didn't look pleased. "I told you to stay in the car! I could have handled a female. You shouldn't have done that!"

"Well, I was only trying to look out for you, don't yell at me! It ain't like I wanted to put my hands on her!" I knew how it felt to be an innocent bystander and I felt like dirt for attacking that woman and Pro chastising me didn't help the situation.

"Well you should have stayed in the fucking car Mesha!"

"MY NAME ISN'T MESHA!" I yelled at him maybe a little too loudly. Pro didn't say anything. His face was red as he drove back to the hotel like a speed racer. Once we arrived back at the hotel, Pro jumped out of the car and slammed the door. I sat in the car like an idiot and cried. With everything that had happened lately, I was a big emotional baby. I just couldn't understand why all this bad stuff was happening. I cried for a good five minutes and then composed myself. When I entered the room, Pro was in the shower. I got on the queen-sized bed closest to the door and closed my eyes.

"You think this a game? Where the money at bitch?!" Crim yelled as he punched and kicked me. I balled up on the floor and tried to shield my face and body from the blows but I was unsuccessful. It hurt so bad that all I could do was scream. "Ty! Ty!!!" I screamed out and that only made Crim laugh, it was a deep, sinister laugh. "Ty ain't here bitch. He left you for dead."

I opened my eyes and realized that I was crying. I sat up, and saw that Pro was getting up out of the bed that he was in. He was shirtless and had on black Polo sweatpants. "What's wrong?" he asked rushing over to the bed.

Embarrassed, I wiped my face with the back of my hands. "A bad dream." I mumbled and sniffed. Pro got up and got a ready rolled blunt and a lighter off the table. He sat down on the bed and passed the items to me. "I have those too. They suck, huh?" he asked as I lit the blunt.

I just nodded. Pro continued. "I be wondering if they gone ever stop. It certainly doesn't make the pain any better, to have to relive the bullshit through dreams." Pro reached over and removed the strands of hair that were stuck to my face from tears and sweat. I gazed at him for a minute and then shifted my eyes to the burgundy carpet, as I inhaled the weed smoke.

"Ty was a shitty boyfriend. He cheated like it was nothing and I had finally decided to leave him for good. I wanted us to co-parent, but I really had no plans of us getting back together, but I miss him like crazy. The crazy thing is, I don't even have any closure. Like where is he? Why hasn't he come back to let me know he was ok or even ask if I was ok?" More tears filled my eyes.

Pro sighed. "I wish I could take your pain away baby girl. I'd never been in love in my life, but Mesha made me fall easy. She was sweet as hell. Innocent, like she was too good for this life. Niggas holla they want a ride or die, but at the end of the day what is it all for? What did she die for?"

Pro stared at the carpet and we were both silent as our own individual thoughts and memories ran through our minds. Once the blunt was gone, I made myself comfortable on the bed.

"You want me to lay with you?" Pro surprised me by asking. I surprised myself even more by nodding my head yes. There was no need to front, I needed to be comforted at the moment and Pro had done a good job so far of making me feel at ease. Pro lay down on the bed and pulled me onto his chest. I lay my head on his chest and listened to his heartbeat. I wasn't sure what we were doing, but it felt right.

I had just closed my eyes when Pro softly called my name. "Bri?"

I looked up at him and was met with a soft kiss on the lips. He had the softest lips. He kissed me again and added tongue. Pro placed his hand on the back of my head and we kissed for a good minute. Pro broke the kiss long enough to pull my shirt over my head and remove my bra.

We switched positions and he got on top of me. My heart rate increased as I anticipated what was coming next. Pro sucked on my neck which drove me absolutely insane because that was my spot. I wrapped one arm around his neck and bit my bottom lip. Pro then gave my nipples attention, alternating between the right and left giving them adequate amounts of pleasure. He then stared into my eyes as he removed my pants and my underwear. I was almost intimidated by his gaze, but I didn't break the eye contact.

Pro got up and removed a condom from the bag that he'd brought with him. I guess men always travel prepared. Once again I waited anxiously. I couldn't miss the monster that he pulled from his boxers but I wasn't scared, Ty had been very well endowed also. I was used to it. I hadn't had sex in a while, so he wasn't able to penetrate me with ease, but when he finally got it in, I gasped and he moaned. He didn't move, he just stayed inside me and kissed me again. After a good fifteen seconds, I couldn't take it anymore. I was soaking wet and started slowly grinding and thrusting. This encouraged him to move. Pro started off with slow steady strokes and then he sped up.

"This shit feel good?" he whispered in my ear and then bit my earlobe.

"Yes." I whimpered on the verge of an orgasm. I wrapped my legs around his waist and found his lips. I kissed him hungrily, moaning into his mouth, as I exploded onto his dick. "Oohhhh shiiittttt." I squealed. Pro lifted my right leg and placed it on his shoulder. His gaze penetrated my soul as he stroked in and out of me. I seemed to get wetter with each stoke. He then flipped me over so that I was flat on my stomach and after a good ten strokes, Pro couldn't take it any longer and he too came inside the condom he was wearing. He lay on top of me for a minute, our heartbeats pounding against our chests. Finally, he kissed me on the lips, and we took turns going into the bathroom to clean up.

I wasn't sure how the sexual encounter would affect our relationship, but that night I slept like a baby snuggled up under Pro. There was no bad dreams and no fear. I knew he was still grieving and in actuality so was I, but I couldn't deny that there was definitely something there.

LET'S DO THIS

Pro

The next day, Bri and I hit the road bright and early. We didn't speak about our sexual encounter, and I wasn't even really sure what it meant but I was feeling shorty. I wasn't ready to make her my girl or anything but I definitely felt the desire to be there for her. She had been though a lot and she was a tough cookie. I respected her gangsta and for some reason, I just wanted to protect her. A part of me felt conflicted like I was betraying Mesha by moving on, but the reality of the situation was she's never coming back.

Surprisingly, our car ride wasn't awkward, despite the spontaneous intimate moment that we had shared. We made small talk that for once didn't revolve around planning robberies, scheming, and murdering. We talked about normal shit like when our birthdays were, our favorite colors, and our favorite movies. It was refreshing to get away from the drama for a few hours, our conversation didn't mention the fact that I'd just killed a man the day before and robbed him of $15,000. I gave Bri $5,000 of the money.

When I pulled up in Bri's driveway is when the awkwardness took over. I wasn't sure if I should hug her or kiss her, ask her out on a date. All of these thoughts ran through my mind as Bri turned in her seat and grabbed her bag from the back of the car. "You working tonight?" I asked. Bri pulled her bag from the back and into her lap.

"Hell no, I'm done with Joe and that club." Bri was looking out of the windshield, as she spoke. Suddenly she squinted her eyes and leaned forward. "What the fuck?" I followed her gaze to see what she was looking at. As I noticed that on the passenger side of Bri's car, her front and rear tires were flat, she opened the door and got out of the car. I got out of the car as well and followed in behind Bri. She got up on her car, and bent down to survey the damage.

"Somebody flattened my fucking tires!"

I looked around the yard and up and down the street and didn't notice anything that seemed out of place. "You beefing with anybody?" I asked, feeling like that was something a female would do.

Bri stood up straight. "Not that I know of. I mean a few bitches might not like me but they have never made any noise. I don't bother anybody, I work and come straight home." Bri said in an agitated manner. Even though I could understand why she was upset, I still made an effort to calm her down.

"Ok ma just breathe. It'll be ok. I'll pay for you to get two new tires." I assured her.

"You don't have to do that Pro." Bri said. "It's not about the money, it's just the principal."

"I know you have the money that has nothing to do with what I just said though. You got triple A?"

Bri nodded her head, attempting to cover up the fact that she was still annoyed.

"Ok, just get them to tow your car to a tire shop." I reached into my jeans' pockets and pulled out a wad of money. I counted off three one hundred dollar bills and handed them to her.

"Pro!" Bri eyed the money and began protesting but I cut her off.

"Take this money, and get some tires. I'll hit you up later." I said in a gentle but assertive tone. Bri reluctantly reached out and took the money and I kissed her on the forehead and left.

I raced towards my own home with my mind going a mile a minute. There had been a string of dramatic events occurring recently on my end as well as Bri's. Joe was a snake and he was a common denominator in some of my grief as well as Bri's but I really didn't think a nigga would slash a females' tires, unless he had some bitch in him.

As I pulled into my own driveway, it didn't take me long to notice that I too had a flat tire and the word bitch had been keyed into the driver door of my Beamer. Disregarding the comforting words that I had just given Bri, my blood began to boil. *Somebody was fucking with us, and the burning question was who?*

A few hours later, I sat in my living room, looking at the 47-inch television that was mounted on the wall above the fireplace. Or rather it was watching me. I wasn't paying any attention to the ratchet reality show that was playing, but was instead plotting. I took a sip of my Henny and coke and pulled a long toke from the burning blunt that I was holding in my left hand. I still had to get at Zoe and I had to handle Joe, and being that Dez was Joe's cousin and possibly linked to the robberies, I may have to get him as well. This was something that required meticulous planning. I couldn't go at it half-assed or I risked the chance of being killed myself or even being caught by the police.

Jock's words plagued my mind as I recalled him saying that Joe had it out for me because I was beginning to come up in the game. It's enough users out here for everybody to eat, but niggas will get on some greedy shit real quick. I also thought back to Bri saying that Ty had a new connect. If Ty decided not to fuck with Joe no more that was a perfect motive for Joe to set him up and since Ty wasn't around to say different and Joe felt Bri didn't know any better it was real easy for him to try and stake claim on any money that Ty may have had. It would also be easy for him to stick me on the niggas and claim that he was owed money so I would split the take with him. I was so glad that I had crossed that nigga and not given him any of the money that I got from Crim. Grimy ass bastard.

My doorbell rang and I immediately grabbed my pistol that sat right beside me on the glass end table. Not too many people knew where I lived and none of them would come by without permission. Paranoia set in as I made my way to the front door. I looked out of the peephole and was shocked to see Stephanie standing on my porch holding a plate in her hands. I had never brought her to my home, we had always had sex at her place. I had certainly never told her where I lived, how in the hell did she know where I rested my head?

I swung my front door open and this broad had the nerve to smile. We hadn't even spoken to each other in days. "Hey Pro. I cooked and I just thought you might like a plate." She stood there like shit was all good, dressed in black leggings and a plain yellow fitted shirt and some yellow flip flops. Her hair was pulled back in a ponytail and even though her stomach still appeared somewhat flat, it looked like her nose had begun to spread a little.

Instead of inviting her inside, I stepped out onto the porch and looked at her like she'd lost her mind. "How do you know where I live?"

At that moment Stephanie glanced down and noticed the pistol I was holding as my arm hung at my side. She glanced back up at me appearing nervous. She shifted her weight from her left leg to the right one. "I, um…one night that I saw you at the club and I um, I followed you after the club. I called and you didn't answer, so I thought you might be going to a girl's house."

I cocked my head slightly to the left and stared at this dummy for a second. She looked normal as hell, but something had to be off with her mental. I looked around as if Ashton was gon' jump out and tell me that I had been *Punked*.

"So let me get this straight. I didn't answer the phone for you, so you followed me? Do you know how psychotic you sound right now, yo? I am not obligated to answer the phone for you and if I was going to see another female it's none of your concern nor your business."

My gaze went from Stephanie's embarrassed face to my car. I stepped closer to her with anger flashing in my eyes. "Did you key my fucking car?"

Stephanie looked terrified. She took a step back. "No, no I haven't touched your car. I'm sorry, I just, and I won't come over here again."

Tears fell from her eyes as she turned around and went down the steps. I stood there watching as she got into her gold Camry and hastily backed out of my driveway. "Crazy bitch." I mumbled to myself.

The next day I made the mistake of riding with Wiz for a few. Even though I made great money riding around the city trapping, I actually get tired of driving. Wiz seemed to use more drugs than he sold and he didn't have a problem with driving me around to make plays since money rarely called his phone. We'd only been riding for a good thirty minutes and I had to point out to the nigga twice that he was speeding. Speeding with drugs in the car was a definite no no. When Wiz picked me up, he appeared real hype and crunk for it to be so early in the morning and I knew right then that he was on a Molly. He popped them like they were candy. I was just about to tell him to take me back to my rental, which was parked in his yard when I heard a siren behind us. I turned around and my heart dropped as I saw blue lights. We were smoking a blunt and I had bundles of heroin in my possession.

I looked at Wiz with an angry expression on my face, "Nigga, I told yo dumb ass to slow down!"

Wiz turned around and looked out of the rearview window. He turned his attention back to the road and seemed to speed up. "Fuck that cracker." He said concentrating on the road. Beads of sweat gathered on his forehead.

My eyes bugged out, I couldn't believe this dude. "You ain't taking me on no gotdamn high speed chase. If yo ignorant ass don't pull this mother fucking car over yo!" I yelled so viciously that spit flew from my mouth.

Wiz drove for a second as if he didn't hear me and then just like that the idiot pulled over. I briefly closed my eyes and shook my head. This was a fucked up day already. There was no doubt in my mind that I was going to jail. The week of Mesha's funeral, I had a court date for a weed charge that I had missed. I was grieving and court was the last thing on my mind. Not to mention the fact that we were smoking and I had heroin, this was just great.

A middle-aged white police officer approached the car and Wiz rolled down the window. "You didn't see my lights back there, son?" the officer asked peering into the car.

"No sir." Wiz said.

"Let me see your license and registration, son." The officer said. Wiz reached over and opened the glove compartment. The officer called for back-up, and waited for Wiz's information. Twenty minutes later, just as I had predicted, we were heading off to the county jail.

I was super pissed because being that Wiz's dumb ass was with me, I didn't have anyone to call to get me out. I trusted my mother but being that she thought I was out of the game I didn't want to lead her to my stash because that would only make her suspicious. I had $45,000 in my safe and nobody was making that kind of money painting. I only needed $4,000 to get out with a bail bondsman, but I knew my parents didn't have that kind of money lying around.

I called Jock and his phone went straight to voice mail. I slammed the phone down angrily as I was led to the holding cell. Once I was inside, I went straight to sleep. Wiz was using the phone and if I saw his face I was liable to choke his ass.

"Prentice William! Let's go." I woke up startled not even aware that I had dozed off. A jailer was at the holding cell door waiting on me to get up. I looked up at the clock and realized that I'd been in the cell for two hours.

I looked over at Wiz who looked just as confused as me. I followed the jailer and waited while she got my jewelry and took me up to the magistrates' office. I saw Bri sitting outside the magistrate's office and was shocked. She was sitting there looking through her phone. Dressed in black jeans, a gray fitted shirt, a black leather biker jacket and black combat boots, she looked sexy as hell. Even dressed casually with no make-up on she was beautiful. Her hair was slicked back in a ponytail and she had on false lashes and clear lip gloss. As I walked into the magistrate's office she looked up and gave me a small smile. I nodded my head as a way of acknowledging her.

It took the magistrate fifteen minutes to go over my charges and to give me information for my court date, tell me what would happen if I miss court again, yadda yadda yadda. After I signed a good ten papers, I was released. I walked out of the office damn near forgetting Wiz.

Bri stood up and I directed her outside before I spoke. "How did you know I was here?"

"I was paying a traffic ticket and saw them bringing in you and your friend. I was scared as hell cause I wasn't sure what they had you for. My cousin is a bail bondsman, and I had him to check it out for me. When I found out what your bond was, I just decided to get you out. I hope you not mad I didn't get your friend but I don't know him or if he good for the money."

"Hell nah I ain't mad, I'll get his stupid ass out even though I should let him sit." Bri smiled and I just stared at her, hypnotized by her beauty. She glanced down at her shoes as if she were embarrassed. I took my pointer finger and lifted her chin up so that she was looking at me.

I stepped closer to her and kissed her on the lips. "Thank you."

She stared into my eyes and whispered, "Anytime."

"Can you take me to my car? I'll go get your money and come back and get dummy." I said.

"Sure."

I didn't have too much to say to Wiz when I bailed him out. As long as he was out here wilding and being reckless, I would handle my business on my own. Taking care of Joe wasn't something that I wanted to do alone, so I recruited Jock to help me with the task. That night we sat across the street from the strip club and waited for Joe to leave. The club didn't close until four a.m., so we went to stake the joint out around three a.m.

At 4:20 a.m. I spotted Joe's new black Porsche pulling out of the club's parking lot. I was baffled as to how his fat ass could even fit in a Porsche. I kept a safe distance, so as not to alert him that he was being followed. Joe drove for seventeen minutes, to a nice neighborhood in the suburbs. He pulled into the driveway of a nice two story home, and I parked a few blocks from the driveway.

Our plan was to ambush him as he was going inside the house. Jock and I quietly emerged from the car, toting sawed off shotguns, and we weren't coming to fuck around. We simultaneously pulled ski masks down over our face and crept up in the yard as Joe and a stripper from his club, headed up the steps. I jogged towards the steps gripping the gun in my hand, as Joe stuck his key inside the door. As soon as my foot hit the first step the female turned around and as soon as she saw two niggas wearing ski masks, holding guns, she screamed. Joe had just twisted the doorknob and he turned around still holding the knob in his hand. His face took on the same wide-eyed expression as his female companion, as I pointed the gun in his face and stepped closer to him. He let the doorknob go, and held up his hands in surrender.

"Inside." I demanded and Joe stepped inside the elaborately decorated house. I held Joe and the stripper at gunpoint, while Jock searched the house for something to secure the female with. I didn't want to kill her, but I needed Joe to see my face before I sent him to hell. Joe stood nervously with his hands up as Jock searched the kitchen. He came back a minute later, holding duct tape in his hand. I pointed my gun in the crying stripper's face. "Get on the floor."

She did as I asked and Jock, taped her hands up behind her back. He then taped her legs together. Once she was secured, I pointed the gun back at Joe. "Upstairs you fat bitch." I instructed.

Joe did as he was told and Jock and I followed him up the stairs and into the master bedroom. Once we entered the room, Joe stopped in the middle of the floor and looked at us helplessly. "There's money in the closet. I swear you don't have to kill me. Just take the money yo. I got kids."

I lifted the ski mask from my face and watched the shock on Joe's face. "Fuck yo kids, nigga. You better be glad I ain't touching them for what you did to my girl. You thought I won't gone find out about yo foul ass huh?" I asked wanting to rip him apart with my bare hands.

"W-w-what you talking about Pro? Come on fam, I told you who..."

I cut him off. "Nigga, fuck all that! You was mad that I was coming up in the game, so you put niggas on me and my girl got touched? Being a greedy bitch ass nigga gon' cost you your life. How it feel knowing you about to die?" I asked cold heartedly. Tears actually began to roll down Joe's face.

"Pro, I had nothing to do with that man. You got to believe me."

I was tired of hearing him talk. "Jock, go in the closet and see what that stash looking like."

Jock headed straight for the closet and I kept my aim steady on Joe. I'm sure that he knew he was a goner and I was enjoying seeing him scared out of his mind. A few minutes later, Jock emerged from the closet carrying two Timberland shoe boxes.

"That's it?" I asked Joe mockingly. "You setting niggas up and orchestrating hits and you don't even have a safe? Two shoeboxes nigga?" before he could respond, I squeezed the trigger and sent Joe flying backwards. The shot knocked him off his feet and he hit the wall and slid down it onto the floor. Being the right-hand man that he was, Jock sent a shot Joe's way and blew half his face off. We grabbed a shoe box each and flew out of the house. When it was all said and done we had $35,000 to split and Joe's grimy ass was no more.

IT'S MY SEASON

Bri

After I bailed Pro out of jail, I had time to just go home and think. It was very odd that Dez had Ty's chain. Yes, Joe was his cousin, but *did Joe just give Dez the chain to try and sell*, I wondered. *Did Syria know anything about who was behind the robbery?* I couldn't bring myself to believe that she would take part in anything like that. *You know who would though,* a small voice said in my head. It was no doubt that my sister was a grimy ass broad and this is exactly something she would take part in. I couldn't jump to conclusions though. Just because she was sleeping with Dez didn't mean that she had to know what he was up to. I chewed on my bottom lip as I thought over every possible scenario in my head. Something was telling me to just talk to her and see if I could get anything out of her. Of course, I would make it seem like I knew more than I actually did. There was a certain way that you had to play Jen.

I got in my car and headed over to her apartment. We hadn't spoken since our argument and I missed my nieces and nephews. That's how cold hearted Jen was, she didn't even reach out to me knowing that my best friend died.

The whole way to Jen's house more and more factors entered my mind. Ty was very particular about people knowing where he stayed. Jen knew and Syria knew, that's it. If things were looking suspect and I had to choose anyone that I believed would have given Dez information, I would choose Jen over Syria any day. The sun had just set when I pulled up in front of the project apartment that Jen lived in. I got out of the car and chirped my alarm. I headed up the sidewalk ignoring the loser ass niggas standing around calling out, "Hey ma" and "Shorty bad." I used my knuckle to tap on Jen's door.

My niece Tia opened the door. Her eyes lit up when she saw me. "Hey." She opened the screen door and threw her arms around my waist. I hugged her back.

"Hey sweetie." I stepped inside the apartment. "Where's your mom?"

"Taking a shower."

I entered the living room and sat down on the couch. "I have to call my dad, but I'll come back and talk to you, okay auntie?"

"Sure thing baby. Where the other kids at?"

"Tyquan's with his friends, the rest are with grandma."

When Tia went into her room, I glanced on the coffee table and saw Jen's phone. My eyes darted towards the bathroom door, and I could hear the shower water running. I anxiously picked up the phone, hoping that Jen didn't have a passcode. I swiped my finger across the screen and couldn't help but smile when I was granted access into her phone.

I scrolled through the text messages, looking for familiar names. The first name I saw was Dez. He was still on the run for murdering Syria. Syria wasn't Jen's friend, but it infuriated me that Jen was talking to this low life ass nigga. I saw that his last text to her read: *I'm gon' send for you when shit blow over. Just hold on.*

So Jen knew where he was. I scrolled up with shaky hands and found a text that caught my eye. Jen had sent it and it read: *My sister and Ty broke up, hit him now while she won't be at the crib.*

I heard the shower turn off as heat radiated through my body. I didn't even want to read anymore. I placed Jen's phone back on the table and tears pooled in my eyes. Jen emerged from the bathroom wrapped in a large, fluffy white towel. I loved my nieces and nephews more than anything in the world and I hated to wild out in front of my niece, but I couldn't control the rage that I was feeling. Whether Ty and I were together or not, I had spent thousands of dollars of his money on Jen and her children in the past. She was the perfect example of a trifling bitch that bites the hand that feeds her. It also didn't matter if Ty and I were supposed to be broken up, because of her scheming and plotting I ended up in something that wasn't even meant for me.

"What are you doing here?" Jen asked peering into the living room. I fixed my gaze on her and all I saw was a low down dirty trifling bitch.

"You helped set up the robbery at Ty's house?" I didn't beat around the bush. I looked her dead in the face and dared her to lie. Jen's mouth dropped open in shock and though she tried her best to pretend that she didn't know what I was talking about, her eyes told it all: she was guilty.

"What are you talking about? Why would I do that?" Jen couldn't even look me in the eyes. Her gaze darted all around the room, she was a bad ass liar.

I was no longer in control of my actions and before I knew it, I had hopped up off the couch and lunged at Jen. She was caught totally off guard as I ran up on her and punched her in the face. I threw punch after punch, and got at least a good four punches in before Jen stopped trying to protect her face and weakly attempted to fight back.

Her towel came off and she was butt ass naked, throwing punches and not even landing half of them. My fist hit her face for the tenth time and blood squirted from Jen's nose. It wasn't until then that I noticed Tia trying to break us up, and her presence snapped me out of my rage.

"Mommy, auntie, stop!" Tia cried.

There was nothing else to say and even through my anger I was low-key embarrassed for behaving like I had in front of my niece. I headed towards the front door, while Jen picked the towel up off the floor and covered herself. Blood or not, I was done with that money-hungry, back stabbing bitch.

The day after my fight with Jen I got on my computer and researched cosmetology schools and apartments in Miami. Now more than ever, I needed a fresh start. Each day I woke up confused still about Ty's disappearance, puzzled about why Joe set everything up the way that he did and now hurt that my own blood played a part in me losing a baby and being brutally beaten. My life had been turned upside down since that night and Jen's messy ass was right in the middle of it. I wanted to kick my own ass for not taking her phone and trying to see if Dez had ever stated his location in any of the messages.

I took a virtual tour of a few apartments, and also applied for two of them. I made plans to enroll in school in the next month. That would give me enough time to get everything taken care of in North Carolina. Pro was cool as hell and our sex had been great, but I had to get out of North Carolina before I lost my mind.

Later that night after showering and putting lavender scented body butter all over, I dressed in a long, flowing white sundress and metallic gold sandals. After I found out about Joe's betrayal, I refused to dance at his club but I still needed a few more thousand dollars to take to Miami. I wasn't playing when I said I wanted to open a high-end salon. That certainly wouldn't be cheap, not to mention that I had to live after I got there. I was going to dance at Teasers, a club thirty minutes away from where I lived. After I applied some make-up and placed curls in my long weave, I grabbed my bag and left the house.

There was a medium sized crowd at the club and after three hours of dancing I had made $450.00 I always made money when the big boys came out. Even if the club was packed, if it was packed with lames, the tips wouldn't be much. All it took was for there to be a good ten ballers present and I could definitely cash out. It was my turn to go up on stage and after assessing the worth of the men in the club, I figured by the time I got off stage, I should have at least $800.00 total. It was crunch time since moving to Miami was only four weeks away for me.

Whenever I got up on stage, I would zone out and try to pretty much block out all of the men in the club and just pretend that it was me and the music. It usually worked. I was actually very shy and it was only my love for money and liquid courage that made it so I was able to strip. My favorite song 'Mile High Club' by Jeremiah was playing. I walked to the edge of the stage and was about to do a sultry dance, when I was yanked off the stage by my arm. I didn't know what in the hell was going on, but I was prepared to have to fight some hating ass bitch. Once I was no longer performing and the lights weren't playing tricks on my eyes, I looked to see who the brave soul was that snatched me off. A security guard rushed over to me just as I recognized the person that had grabbed me and all the color drained from my face, it was Ty.

YOUR TURN

Pro

Of the group of men who'd violated me, Zoe was the family man. As I sat outside his house in the UPS van, I watched as his eight year old daughter played on the front porch of the home. As I did, I was reminded as to why I didn't have kids.

Out of my entire life, Mesha was the only person I could say I ever actually *loved*. I *had* love for people. But *having* love and actually *loving* someone are two different things. The hurt of losing someone you *have* love for can be gotten over. But the hurt of losing someone you *love* is one that can stick with you forever, a pain that keeps your sleep filled with nightmares and your heart filled with regret. It was torture.

I had never quite let a person get so close to me that I could say I loved them until Mesha. Before her I had never wanted to invest emotions into anything or anyone that I wasn't willing to leave at the drop of a dime if shit in my line of work called for it. I had to be that way. Niggas out here will hurt what you love in order to get to you. They'll *kill* what you love in order to get to you. I always knew that. That's why I chose not to have kids. I knew losing a child would destroy me. I'd never be able to function again, let alone live.

Mesha, I have to admit, had me entertaining having kids. Shit, she had me entertaining a lot of things; even contemplating leaving the game. It is what it is. For her I would've done anything.

Returning to reality, I watched the girl continue to play on the porch. I sighed as I did. Dread filled me. I hated to bring a man's wife and child into retribution but in this case I had no choice. After what Reggie had told me just before I murked him in his house, there was no other way around it.

Zoe had to pay the same price he had made me pay.

I pulled the Beretta from underneath the seat and stared at it with no words said. Obviously, guns were nothing new to me. They were tools of my trade, tools that my life often relied on. At the current moment, though, for the first time I actually thought about the damage a gun could do, the futures it could end.

Raising my eyes from it to the little girl again, I sighed knowing the damage to come.

Tucking the gun, slipping on my sunglasses and hat, I stepped out of the van and into the evening dressed in a UPS uniform. Casually looking around me at my surroundings and seeing no one sitting on their porches, I placed the clipboard underneath my arm, closed the door, made my way around the front of the van and headed up the walkway. Reaching the porch's steps, I asked the child if her mother was home.

"Yes," she replied innocently.

"Can you get her for me?"

Nodding, she ran into the house eagerly.

Heading up the steps, once again I sighed. Damn, what a career I had chosen for myself. Now standing outside the door, I developed a stone expression and told myself that just like the other murders I had recently committed, this one was just as necessary.

"Can I help you?" Ariel asked opening the door, her daughter beside her.

"Yes, is Alonzo Carter in?" I asked using Zoe's government name. "I've got a delivery for him."

"He's not here right now. I'm his wife. I can sign for it."

"Signing for it won't be necessary, ma'am," I told her letting the clipboard slide from underneath my arm and fall to the floor of the porch. A second later, the Beretta was in my hand and pointing directly in her face, its nozzle against her forehead.

Going into and immediate panic, Ariel's eyes widened as she quickly reached for her daughter and shoved her behind her in an attempt to shield her from gunfire. "Just don't hurt my baby," she pleaded. "Whatever you want. Just please don't hurt my baby."

Forcing my way in, my gun still to her head, I told her as she stumbled backwards nearly knocking her daughter down, "Fuck all that. Where's Zoe?"

"I...I...I don't know," she stuttered.

The little girl held tightly to her mother as she peeked from behind her with fear in her innocent eyes.

Click-Clack!

I cocked the gun.

Panic and fear both became understatements for the expression on Ariel's face. I could see how hard and fast she was breathing. I could see her tense. I could see sheer terror in her eyes. Squeezing the handle of the gun, my trigger finger tensing, I said, "I want Zoe here. And I want him here soon. If he's not here, you and your daughter are dead."

Beginning to cry, she said still stuttering, "I...I...have to call him."

"Then get to callin', bitch!"

With that yelled at her, I shoved her away from her daughter, slammed the door, and placed the gun to the child's head.

"Not my baby," Ariel pleaded from the floor. Her entire world looked like it was collapsing. Her eyes were expressing it.

"Make the call!"

"Okay, alright," she said quickly. Getting up off the floor she headed to the table in front of the couch, grabbed her iPhone and began to call, her hands trembling. As she did, she looked at her child trying to tell her with her eyes that everything would be okay. Obviously, though, in her heart, she wasn't sure if it was the truth or a lie.

"And act like you got some sense. Act normal. Just tell him you need him here now."

She nodded quickly.

"And, Ariel?"

"Yes?"

Jabbing the gun so forcefully against the little girl's head that it had to tilt towards the opposite side, I said, "Try anything slick, and I'll put a hole yo' baby's head big enough to drive a truck through."

Even I could fee Ariel's heart and stomach plunge.

The wait had only been a half an hour so far but it seemed like an eternity. Sitting in the chair, I kept my eyes on both Ariel and the baby. Honestly, I felt like shit. My conscience was nagging at me like crazy. That had never happened. But then again, I had never been in a position like this one before.

Silence.

The passing of minutes.

As I sat there clutching the gun, I thought about how I had made the mistake of calling Bri, Mesha the night we were headed back to the motel after I had killed Reggie. I had called her that because Mesha was on my mind. Of course she had been on my mind constantly since her death. But after stepping over Reggie's bloody body and darting out the door, she was on my mind even more so because of what he'd told me before I killed him. Now she was on my mind again intensely. But strangely, Bri was also.

I liked Bri. There was no doubt about that but I was now wondering if it was just out of mourning or if it was truly genuine. I wasn't sure if it was out of vulnerability. I did know though the two of us had both lost someone special to us and it had us connecting, connecting in a way that I wasn't too quick to walk away from. But damn. Just like Mesha was my weakness, it scared me to know if I let Bri in, she could become my weakness also.

A car door slammed outside.

"Daddy!" the little girl yelled.

Pulling her child close to her, Ariel glanced at me.

Getting up from the couch, I headed across the living room to the window and peeked out the curtains to see Zoe quickly headed across the lawn, his car behind him in the driveway. Quickly, I hid on the opposite side of the door and waited for him to come inside.

Seconds passed briefly.

Footfalls on the porch.

A key entered the lock.

The doorknob turned.

I clutched the gun tightly. In my mouth I could literally *taste* my revenge. I could feel it. I could see it. The other murders leading up to now satisfied my yearning for payback but this one right here was going to go *beyond* just satisfaction. It was much deeper.

The door opened.

Zoe entered the living room. Seeing Ariel and his baby sitting on the floor, he saw tears in their eyes. "What happened?" he asked. "What's going on?"

"I happened, nigga," I told him placing the gun to the back of his skull.

Zoe froze, his eyes still locked on his family.

Shutting the door behind me, I told him, "Surprise, nigga."

"What the fuck, man? What do you want?"

Forcing him around, I asked, "Ain't it obvious?"

His eyes widened as he immediately recognized me.

The two of us stared into each other's eyes.

Knowing exactly why I was there, Zoe quickly said, "My family ain't got nothin' to do wit' this."

"My girl had nothin' to do wit' it neither. She didn't have a *fuckin'* thing to do wit' it, remember, nigga?"

Zoe silenced. His eyes were speaking though. They expressed fear. But not for himself. It was more so for his wife and child. He knew what he had done. But most importantly, he knew it warranted the forfeiture of his family's lives.

"Just before I murked Reggie he told me you were the one who squeezed the trigger," I said.

Zoe didn't speak.

"You had the money. You had what you came for, muthafucka. But you still shot my girl down like a dog in the street."

Zoe still couldn't say a word.

"You know the rules of the game, nigga," I told him. "You invade my house, I invade yours."

Ariel and her daughter were whimpering.

With a swat, I dropped Zoe to the floor with the butt of the gun. His temple split open widely and easily. Blood trickled from it down the side of his face.

Ariel cried harder. Her child clung to her even tighter than before.

I headed across the floor to both of them and aimed the gun.

"No!" Zoe yelled, tears in his eyes.

"A life for a life, nigga!" I yelled back.

"Don't do this, man!"

"You did it to yourself!"

"Please!"

I placed the gun to Ariel's head.

"Mommy!" the little girl screamed fearfully as she buried her face in her mother's chest.

"Man, I'm the one who killed your girl!" Zoe screamed. "I did that. Me, nigga. My wife ain't got shit to do wit' it. Kill me, nigga!"

Ignoring him, I cocked the slide.

The little girl pulled herself closer to her mother's body, embracing her like it would be the very last time she would feel her body.

Ariel's eyes were closed tightly as she held her baby. Tears were escaping from her closed lids and streaming down her cheeks. She had never been more scared of anything before in her life.

Amid Zoe's pleading, I saw Mesha's face in my head. I heard her laughter. I smelled her perfume. With all of those things running through my mind, heart and soul, I squeezed the trigger.

Crack!

"Nooooooooooooo!" Zoe screamed.

Ariel's body slumped quickly to the floor and fell on its side but it seemed like it was falling in slow motion. Half her head and face had torn away from her neck. Her arms, which were holding her daughter, dropped at her sides limply.

She lay there dead.

I turned to Zoe.

Zoe stared at his wife. The same regret my eyes possessed when I had discovered Mesha dead were now the same his possessed. The same pain and torment written on my face was the same now written on his.

Covered in blood, the child stood from her mother and dashed across the floor to her dad crying. He was all she had left in this world. The two now held each other.

I aimed the gun at Zoe's face.

"Don't kill my daddy," the child pleaded.

Her voice tugged at my heart. I hated to have to do what I needed to do right in front of her eyes but there was no way around it. Things were the way they were. Her father had brought about this moment.

Zoe couldn't speak. He was defeated. Holding his baby, he could only look up into the barrel of the gun with tears in his eyes.

Seconds passed.

Then…

I squeezed.

Zoe fell on his back, his left eye replaced with a gaping hole in its socket, his body sounding like a sack of bricks as it hit the floor. Blood poured down his face and out the back of his head. Underneath him it pooled and spread soaking the carpet, its stench fresh, its color crimson.

I stood there for a moment with the gun still aimed, smoke slithering from its barrel. I couldn't move as I watched the child cry and beg her father to wake up.

Moments passed.

Finally, I turned and headed for the door, two dead bodies serving as my backdrop. Amidst the child's whimpering, I opened the door and headed out into the evening quickly realizing the living room had me feeling caged in. Reaching the van, I hopped inside and tossed the gun onto the passenger seat. Seconds later, I pulled away from the curb. As I drove, I began to feel nauseous. Killing a child's parents right in front of her wouldn't leave me.

Seconds later, I had no choice but to pull over to the curb, open the door and throw up.

TWISTS AND TURNS

Bri

For nearly an hour the water cascaded down my body from the shower's chrome nozzle. The enclosing glass sweated and steam filled both the shower and the master bedroom. As it did, I stood with the palms of my hands flat against the wall, one foot extended ahead of me, my head down, my eyes closed. Seconds later, I opened my eyes to look down at my stomach. Taking my hands from the wall and placing them on my belly, it was still so difficult to accept that just a short time ago there was a life inside, a living breathing person, a life and person that I had been looking so forward to being a huge influence on. I'd tried my best to move past the loss. Now I was realizing I most likely never would.

Moments passed.

My mind was filled with a million different thoughts and emotions, most dark and sharply thorned. There were regrets. There was anger. There was bitterness. There was darkness. No matter what, though, they were all revolving around one person...

Ty.

After finishing my shower, I stepped out, put on my white Chanel robe, wrapped my towel around my hair and headed across the marble floor to the master bedroom. In it I was greeted by towering two-storied windows that exposed a breathtaking lake view, a gorgeous night sky above it. Ignoring it, I headed to the satin sheeted bed, sat down and stared at the carpeted floor surrounded by wages of wealth: towering ceiling, huge walk in closet, chandelier, vanity table and chair, and more. None of it meant anything to me. The fifteen hundred dollar evening dress sprawled out beside her and the heels beneath it on the floor didn't even seem to exist to me.

Silence.

Once again, I thought about my child. I thought about what led up to his death. I thought about being left on my own to deal with it. Hatred began to build as I slid a leg underneath myself.

Nothing else around me seemed to exist at the moment; not the countless Gucci shopping bags, Fendi purses, the boxes of Prada heels, *nothing*. If anything, all those things nauseated me to the damn tenth power. Because who they had come from, they were a reminder of the loss of my baby.

Ty walked into the bedroom dressed in a pair of black Tom Ford dress pants, Barker Black loafers, and a white button down dress shirt; suspenders over its shoulders. "You ain't dressed yet, baby?" he asked kissing me on the cheek.

By reflex, I pulled away from the kiss and refused to give eye contact. Its feel on my flesh sickened me. Shit, the scent of his body, that scent that once used to make my pussy wet, now sickened me. I honestly didn't even want him near me.

Seeing my reaction, Ty paused for a moment, staring down at me. A brief moment later, he said, "Got cha somethin'."

My eyes were still down. Whatever he'd bought me, I didn't care. Since he'd snatched me out of the club two nights ago, he'd been splurging on me. He'd definitely been making some big moves during our separation. I didn't care though. Nothing he bought could change how I now felt about him.

Opening a small black bag, Ty pulled out a black box with *Jacob The Jeweler*'s imprint on it and said, "Thought this would look beautiful around your wrist tonight."

I still didn't raise my eyes from the floor.

Opening the box, Ty revealed a platinum bracelet laced with countless diamonds. With the light from the chandelier colliding with their sparkle, the diamonds looked as if they were dripping from the platinum.

"Beautiful, ain't it?"

"Yeah, whatever," I said dryly, barely even giving the bracelet a glance.

Sighing, Ty shut the bracelet box and said, "What the fuck, Bri?"

I ignored him. His presence, let alone just the sound of his voice, was getting underneath my skin.

"This bracelet cost me nearly ten racks," he said.

"I didn't tell you to buy it," I told him as I stood and headed across the room to the window. I just couldn't take too much more of being that damn closed to him.

"Bri, I know you're mad but you're actin' spoiled right now."

In disbelief at what I had just heard him say, I turned from the window; the lake outside as my backdrop. "You got the fuckin' nerve to talk about how *I'm* acting?"

He sighed with annoyance and rolled his eyes while carelessly tossing the Jacob box on the bed. "Here we go again," he said.

"You leave me to die in that house, but you got the fuckin' nerve to complain about how *I'm* acting? How 'bout how the fuck *you're* acting, Ty? You're trying to act like the shit didn't happen. For the past two days you've been expecting me to just get over the shit."

"Hell yeah I'm expecting you to get over it because it's done. It's over. We got a new life now. A new house. A new everything."

Putting my hands on my hips, I asked, "Oh, is that it? You buy me some expensive shit and that's supposed to change the fact that you left me like a coward?"

His eyes narrowed. "Watch your mouth. I told you why I left. I knew they weren't going to kill you. I've been in this game long enough. I knew they just wanted the money. They weren't going to kill you. You're alive, ain't you?"

"But my Goddamn child is dead!" I screamed at him. "My child is gone!"

"We'll have more children, Bri. There's plenty of time for that. You know I want a family with you."

"I can't tell."

"How you gon' say some shit like that?"

"Because a father doesn't just up and leave his family the way you did."

He shook his head.

I stood there seething at him.

"I'm sorry," he said. "I told you I had to lay low until I could figure out who was who and what was what. I was just as mixed up about that night as you were. I didn't know who to trust."

"So you didn't even trust me. You left me."

"But I watched you. I was always watching you. That's how I knew you were workin' in that club."

Pissed, I said, "Well, I wish you would've left me there."

"You're my girl. And my girl don't strip like no hoe."

"Oh, you of all people got judgment for a muthafucka?"

"Bri, we don't have time for this shit. The reservations for the restaurant are in an hour. Get dressed."

"I ain't goin'."

"Fuck you mean you ain't goin'?"

"What I just said. I ain't goin'."

"Goddamnit!" he yelled. "I told you I apologize."

"Like an apology can get back the child I lost."

He paused for a moment.

Silence.

Cocking his head to the side, he said, "I know what this shit is really about. It's about that nigga."

Looking at him like he'd lost his mind, I asked, "What nigga?"

"Told you I had been watchin' your ass. This is about that nigga you were runnin' around wit' while I was out the picture."

"What?"

"Yeah, didn't think I knew?"

Shaking my head, I said, "You know what? I can't do this with you. I can't even be around you anymore."

With that said, I walked passed Ty to the dresser, opened a drawer and began to take out an outfit.

"Fuck you doin'?" he asked.

"Leaving."

"What the Hell are you talkin' about?"

"I'm done, Ty. We're done. I don't know why I even let you get me to this house."

I snatched off my robe and began to slide into a set of bra and panties.

Grabbing my arm and forcing me around, he said, "We're not done, Bri."

Snatching away, I yelled, "Don't touch me!"

"I'm tryin' to talk to you."

"You leave me like a coward and got the nerve to think you can just pop back up into my life?"

He grew angry at what he'd just been called. "I told you a minute ago to watch yo' mouth," he said. "Chill wit' that coward shit."

"Fuck you."

Smack!

The open handed slap collided with flesh so loudly it sounded like a gunshot.

I stood there in surprise for a moment holding my face. The vision in my left eye was blurry. For a moment I was seeing two of Ty. My brain seemed scrambled. Ty had never hit me. He had never put his hands on me. I couldn't believe he had just done it.

"I told you about your fuckin' mouth, bitch," he said.

I was absolutely speechless. I couldn't believe he'd just called me a bitch. He'd never called me out my name before. Who the Hell was this man? It was like the very last time I saw him before the gunshots that night, he was Ty. Now, he was a complete stranger, someone I had never met.

We glared at each other.

Finally...

Still holding my face, I said, "I'm definitely leaving now."

With that said, I shoved passed him.

Grabbing my wrist and jerking me towards him like a rag doll, Ty asked, "What the fuck do you think this is? A Democracy, hoe? You think you have a choice?"

Feeling like my wrist was going to break, I said as I grimaced in pain, "Ty, you're hurting my damn wrist."

He applied more pressure and said, "The fuck you mean you gon' leave me? Bitch, you don't decide when you gon' leave me. I decide when I'm gon' leave *you*!"

Feeling more pressure being applied to my wrist, pain shot up the entire length of my arm. I was down on nearly one knee in agony. "Ty, you're hurting me!"

"That's the point, bitch."

With me now down completely on both knees in immense pain and with tears falling from my eyes, he said, "Let's get one thing straight… You don't run shit 'round here. I'm the bread winner. I'm your man. That means my word is what counts around this muthafucka, understood?"

"Yes, yes," I said quickly, more tears streaming.

"We gon' put the past behind us. I don't want to hear another thing about that night. And I definitely don't want to hear another muthafuckin' thing about you leavin' me. You hear me?"

"Yes," I told him. It felt like my arm was about to snap right out of the socket. I honestly thought that was his intention.

"Do you hear me?!" he yelled.

"Yes!" I screamed.

Finally letting my wrist go, he glared down at me for several moments as I sat there in my bra and panties holding my wrist. He then said, "Put some makeup on your face to cover that bruise and get dressed. I told you we got reservations and I ain't wasting my damn money."

With that said, he turned around and headed for the door. As he did, he stopped at the vanity, went in my purse and grabbed my phone. Stuffing it in his back pocket, he opened the door.

I glared evilly at Ty's back. No man had ever hit me. I thought about Syria and what had happened to her. I would be damned if I was going to let that happen to me. I would be damned if I was going to be some man's punching bag.

Stepping into the hallway and turning to me, Ty said, "Oh, and about that punk ass nigga you were fuckin' wit' while I was gone. I suggest you get him out your head. He's going to be out of commission for a while. Shit, in fact, he's gonna be out of commission for a long, long time. You best believe that shit."

With that said, he was gone.

Sitting on the floor in pain and crying while holding my wrist, and with no phone to make a call, I could only wonder what he meant about Pro.

PLOTTING FOR REVENGE

Bri

It was nearly twelve in the afternoon as I stood in the mirror of the bathroom staring at my face. The entire left side was bruised and swollen from the slap. My head was even aching. Shaking my head in anger, I was pissed. I needed 'get back' but didn't quite know how I was going to go about getting it.

I hadn't slept too good last night. Lying beside Ty, all I could think about was how quickly he'd gone from someone I had loved to someone I despised. At dinner he acted like putting his hands on me wasn't something serious. It seemed passive to him. He never even apologized. Then when dinner was over and we were back home, he actually had the nerve to think he was going to get some pussy. I shut that down, obviously. As far as I was concerned, he'd never get inside me again.

Heading out of the bathroom, I stopped and looked out the window at the beautiful view from the living room window. Seeing boats off in the distance underneath the sun, I wondered what was going on with Pro. I couldn't get what Ty had said out of my head. I was worried about Pro. But since Ty had taken my phone and still hadn't given it back, there was no way for me to find out if Pro was okay.

During the little bit of sleep I did manage to get last night, I dreamed about Pro. I dreamed about the night we had made love. I dreamed about his touch, his voice. Even now at the current moment I could smell him. When I woke up last night, though, after those pleasurable escapes from reality, I awakened to Ty's arm wrapped around my body. I swear his touch had me sick to my fucking stomach. I tried to squirm out from under his arm but he stirred and tightened his grip. From that point, I pretty much spent the entire night lying there on my back staring up at the ceiling.

As I now stood at the window, my hands against its surface, I knew my current life wasn't the life for me. The money, the cars, being the drug dealer's girl; those things weren't for me, at least not if that drug dealer was Ty. I couldn't do it. But for now,

I had no way out. I would have to deal with it until I could figure out a way to leave him.

Sliding my feet into my house shoes, still wearing my robe, I left the bedroom and made my way down the split staircase. Reaching the bottom, I headed towards the kitchen. Not seeing Ty, I was satisfied. But yet something had me needing to know where he was. Seconds later, I headed to his den. Approaching it, I could hear voices. Placing my ear to the door, I could hear a conversation.

"When is it going to be done?" Ty's voice asked.

"Shit, the wheels are already in motion," another voice said.

"You sure?"

"Yeah."

"If I've wasted my money, there are goin' to be serious consequences, bruh. I don't play 'bout my money."

"I feel you. Trust me; everything's taken care of. Like I said, the wheels are in motion, right now, as we speak. I got this."

"Good, because I don't ever want to see that nigga's face again. Muthafuckas can't touch my woman and think it's cool."

I placed my ear tightly to the door.

"I feel you," the stranger's voice said.

As I listened, I couldn't recognize the voice of the man Ty was talking to but I figured they were talking about the night of the robbery and shooting. I figured Ty was now planning revenge.

The voices lowered.

I pressed my ear as tightly to the door as possible, listening intently. As minutes passed, I couldn't quite hear much. Everything now seemed low and muffled.

"Shit," I said in frustration.

Moments passed.

Then...

"Jock, I'm payin' you good money, nigga. Make sure this gets done right."

Hearing the name Jock, I paused for a moment. I remembered Pro mentioning that name before. It was a friend of his who had told him about Joe and his involvement in both Pro's robbery and Ty's. *What the fuck? How did Jock know Ty?*

Footfalls sounded behind the door.

Hearing both men now heading towards the door, I quickly headed to the kitchen. Reaching the kitchen, I opened the refrigerator, pulled out some food and acted like I was getting ready to prepare a lunch.

Voices came from the foyer.

Seconds passed.

No longer hearing voices, I headed to the window and peeked through the blinds to see Ty and Jock standing beside

Jock's black E-Class Mercedes Sedan. I couldn't tell what they were talking about despite how hard I tried to read their lips. Then seeing Ty glance towards the kitchen window, I quickly dipped back and closed the blinds. A second later, I was back at the island preparing lunch.

The foyer's door closed.

Ty walked into the kitchen and headed to the refrigerator without giving me eye contact, the soles of his Gators clicking along the floor's surface. Grabbing a bottled water, he opened it and leaned against the sink staring at me from behind. Feeling his eyes on me, I kept preparing lunch. Seconds later, I turned and headed to the sink. Reaching it and turning on the water, his eyes were still on me.

Then…

"Bri?"

"Yeah?" I answered while refusing to look at him.

"I meant what I said last night about you never leaving me," he said. He then grabbed my chin, forced my face towards him and said, "If you ever try, I'll kill you."

Silence fell between us.

He stared into my eyes. His glare was menacing and sent chills down my spine. Just like last night, he seemed like a stranger to me. But stranger or not, his words scared the shit out of me. The fact that he seemed like a stranger made them all the more scary. Since I didn't quite know this stranger…

He might really keep his word.

Letting go of my chin, he left the kitchen.

Standing at the sink, I couldn't move. I couldn't speak. My body was trembling. I had never been a scary bitch but, damn, Ty's change had me uneasy. It was then as I stood there that I realized the conversation in the den wasn't about plotting revenge for the robbery…

It was about doing something to Pro.

WHO CAN I TRUST?

Pro

It was early afternoon as I got dressed and prepared to make some rounds and check some traps. A nigga couldn't make any money in bed. That had always been my mentality. Now dressed, I grabbed my phone and glanced at the missed calls and texts, most revolving around transactions. There were many but not a single one from Bri. I wondered about that.

Over the past several days I thought about Bri. I thought about all she'd gone through. All she'd lost. But through it all, she still managed to remain flawless. She was a strong woman. I admired that. We were similar in that way. I enjoyed thinking about her.

Sighing, I didn't quite know what to do about her. I couldn't get her off my mind. I definitely was feeling her. But at the same time, the love of my life was still on my mind heavy, the woman I'd lost. My policy of never getting too involved with someone you couldn't leave behind was weighing on my mind also. Obviously, I'd ignored that policy before and was paying for it in heavy regret, sleepless nights, a broken heart, and bloody nightmares. That shit was absolute torture.

Life was complicated, I learned. A nigga didn't want to be alone, didn't want to die in the gutter or in a nursing home with no family, no kids, no grandkids; body ravaged by some debilitating disease. I'd seen that happen to far too many old heads. The shit was super depressing. But at the same time, a nigga didn't want to spend his life lonely. Shit, there was only so much happiness money and cars could provide. And although pussy could be gotten at any time, there was absolutely nothing in the world like having a good woman at home waiting for you with a hot meal cooked, a woman who could be trusted, a woman who was only yours.

I was torn.

Standing in my living room for a while, I finally swiped my finger across its touchscreen and called Bri. I didn't know if it was the right thing. I had my worries and doubts. But I guess only time was going to tell if I was making the right decision. I just hoped it wasn't the type of decision that would leave me in pain. Listening and anticipating the sound of her voice, I heard it alright. But it wasn't her *actual* voice. It was the voice of her voicemail. Disappointed, I left a message for her to call me and ended the call.

It was about ten minutes later as I headed to the door to get out into the streets. Approaching the door, my cell rang. Recognizing the ringtone, I answered, "Yo."

"You at the house?" Jock asked, the sound of traffic in the background.

"Yeah, but 'bout to go check on some money. Got a busy day ahead of me."

"I'm right around the corner. Don't go anywhere yet. I got some shit you really need to know about. I'll be there in five minutes."

"A'ight."

"I'm for real, Pro. Don't leave. It's important."

"I got cha. I'll be here."

The call ended.

Sliding the phone back into my pocket, I went to the kitchen to grab a Heineken out of the refrigerator and wait on Jock. Cracking it open, I took a sip and headed back to the living room.

One minute passed.

Two passed.

Ten.

Fifteen.

Wondering what was holding Jock up, I called him. With the phone to my ear, I listened to it ring. Then I got his voicemail. "Yo, bruh, where you at?" I asked. "I got shit to do. Hit me."

I ended the call.

Where the hell was this nigga, I wondered? Why hadn't he answered the phone? With those questions on my mind, a weird feeling enveloped me. It was like a sixth sense sort of feeling. It didn't feel right. It was the type of feeling I got just before I entered the house to discover my queen murdered. Putting my beer down, I headed to the window and peeped out the curtains. When my eyes saw what was outside, it became obvious why my sixth sense was bugging me.

Unmarked cars were parked along my curb and in my driveway. There were at least two dozen of them. Two white vans with tinted windows were parked also. Dozens of cops in jeans, sneakers and bullet proof vests were quickly headed across my lawn towards the porch with their guns drawn.

"Shit," I said nervously and in surprise.

Backing away from the window and almost stumbling over my own feet, I now stood in the center of the living room with my heart racing and my adrenaline pumping. Everything was spinning. My body was trembling from head to toe. I had no idea what to do. Quickly, I darted to the kitchen and looked out the window to see more cops converging.

"Fuck!"

Countless visions of prison bombarded me from all directions, a place I had always said I would never go, a place that always seemed like the type of place dumb niggas went for making the most asinine mistakes, not niggas like me.

Seconds passed by blindingly.

My heart pumped.

All I could do was stand there in the kitchen, with a million different thoughts flooding through my mind. One in particular, though, stood out from them all…

Had Jock had set me up or was this just a coincidence?

PART 2
COMING SOON!

WAIT...DON'T GO!

Here's a few chapters from

FILTHY RICH: PART 1

by: Kendall Banks

Dedication

This book is dedicated to my readers. I owe a debt of gratitude to you for your love and continuous support. Thank you from the bottom of my heart.

Acknowledgements

Thank you to everyone who has inspired me, influenced me, or contributed to my success as an author in any way. Writing a book is a long journey and hard work…actually no matter how many books you write, it never gets easier. I consider myself extremely blessed to be a part of such an amazing team (LCB). A special thanks will forever go to Tressa "Azarel" Smallwood. Thanks for believing in me many years ago and thanks for enthusiastically supporting all of my new projects. There are not enough words to express my gratitude for everything you've done. To my entire family…you've given me more support than I could ever imagine and for that I love you for life!!!

Love,
Kendall Banks
Facebook: /authorkendallb
Twitter: @authorkendallb
Instagram: authorkendallb

Dear Diary

Tonight was on the money…The sex was great…The tongue even better.

Still…my boo better step up. The stakes are getting higher. He promised to get all my needs fulfilled. It's just not coming fast enough.

CHAPTER 1

Her build was slim but curvaceous and athletically toned...her stomach washboard smooth. She was the woman most men craved. With long, jet-black, silky weave draping below her shoulders she seemed perfect...like a sweet, petite goddess. Her light brown skin and thick lips made her assailants second guess their mission. After all, she was supposed to be family.

She was beautiful.

Her beauty couldn't be seen though at this particular moment. It was buried deeply underneath pain, bruises, scars, cuts, blood and tears. She looked nothing like the woman she had always prided herself on being.

Nessa's weave now had no body or shape. It was now heavily matted and dangled wildly over her entire blemished face. Her left eye was swollen and completely shut while her right eye contained semi-blurred vision. Her nose felt like it was broken, making it difficult for her to breathe as blood poured endlessly from both nostrils. Yet she never whined or complained. Her lips were swollen, dry and cracked while blood ran from the slit in her bottom lip. Her fingernails were missing; torturously ripped from her fingers with pliers by her captors. There was absolutely no beauty left to her.

Nessa's body was now as weak as that of a newborn baby. She had no fight left in her and couldn't stand on her own as the two gunmen dragged her stumbling through the dark woods. Overhead, beams of moonlight dimly illuminated the path in front of them. Her bare feet were becoming more and more soiled with dirt while her sweat soaked her body and clothes. Broken branches snapped underneath them while also piercing her soles so deeply they drew blood, too.

"All you had to do was talk, bitch," one of the goons told her.

He was dressed in a wife beater that exposed his muscular arms covered from wrist to shoulder in gruesome looking scars. Wearing a pair of crispy blue Dickies that sagged his Polo boxers were exposed. On his feet were a pair of white Shell-toed Adidas. In his free hand was a chrome Glock that he intended on using to destroy Nessa for good.

"Yeah, bitch," the gunman on Nessa's left side belted, agreeing with his partner. He was just as muscular as the other man but more thuggish. In his free hand was a black .45 that he'd suddenly decided to press against Nessa's head.

"Got to hand it to you though," he continued. "You're a strong one; real strong. Most bitches fold after only a minute. You got balls, bitch. "

"Hell yeah," the other agreed.

"You though, you hung in there. You went out like a soldier."

Their voices werc dripping with sarcasm, not admiration.

Nessa was nearly drifting in and out of consciousness as the men spoke to her. The pain nearly killed her. It was torture. Making her actually wish and yearn for death as she drifted into unconsciousness again. Her mind played back everything from the moment her captors caught her.

The two men had caught Nessa coming out of the hair salon. As she hit the unlock button on the key to her tinted out black Range Rover, a white cargo van emerged out of nowhere and skidded to a stop behind her. Before she could react its side door slid open and two masked men jumped out. In the blink of an eye they had her in their arms with a hand over her mouth and tossed her inside. The next several hours were the most brutal and terrifying she'd ever experienced or endured.

"Where the fuck Luke's stash houses at?" was one of the questions Nessa was asked over and over again.

"Fuck you!" she returned countless times, even spitting in one of the captors' face once when he got too close.

Nessa wasn't weak. She wasn't soft. She had a past full of violence and had crazy survival skills. She'd been born and bred to be loyal. The term "Death Before Dishonor" meant something special to her. She even had it tattooed in old English letters across her bikini line. For her, those words weren't just a phrase. They were a way of life, especially when it came to the most important man in her life...

Luke.

Luke and his family were the most successful crime family Washington D.C. had ever seen. They were a family of multimillionaires who ran each of their *enterprises with an iron fist. Disrespect wasn't tolerated. Fear among their soldiers wasn't accepted. Talking to the police was a mandatory death sentence.*

They weren't a joke.

Nessa was Luke's heart. She was both his queen and princess. He kept a plush roof over her head and her pockets loaded. The rare diamonds around her wrists and neck couldn't be rivaled by many. Luke had real money...old and new. He kept the most expensive clothes and fabrics on Nessa's skin and the newest designer heels and sandals on her pedicured feet.

He loved her but beyond measure.

It was because of that love that Nessa would never tell on him or his family. She didn't care who was asking. It didn't matter if those infiltrators were killers or the Feds themselves. She'd die before turning over on Luke. And during the current moment, it looked like dying was exactly what she was going to do.

For hours in the dirty basement that smelled of mildew and piss, the torture and abuse continued. As a light bulb dangled by a thin wire from overhead, she was beaten, choked, slapped, kicked and spat on. All of it

occurred as she sat helpless in a wooden chair with her
wrists and ankles duct taped to it.

"Talk, bitch!" one of the men yelled just before
punching her in the face so hard she thought her jaw was
broken. "Where the fuck his stash houses at?"

Dazed and barely able to lift her chin from her
breasts, she said weakly, "Eat a dick, bitch!"

Looking at his partner, the goon laughed and said,
"Whoaaaaaaaaaaa, she's got balls. Eat a dick, huh?"

With her chin in her chest and looking up at him
through her matted hair and swollen eye, she said, "What,
you deaf, muthafucka? Yeah, I said eat a dick."

The two men laughed again. One of them then
unzipped his pants, freed his dick and said, "Naw, bitch.
How 'bout you drink some piss?" He then began to
urinate all over her. By the time he was finished, piss had
drenched her weave and tank top. Its stench smelled so
bad she threw up all over the floor.

"We can do this all night, bitch," he told her as he
placed his dick back in his pants and zipped up. "I don't
have any place to be. And you just might get raped in this
muthufucka if you don't talk soon."

148

Several moments passed by. Nessa feared getting raped but still remained silent. Soon, more punches battered Nessa's face.

"Talk, ho!" the gunman demanded as he struck Nessa in the stomach.

Coughing and gasping for air, Nessa said, "Okay, okay, I'll...I'll..."

"You'll what?" he asked, pressing his ear close to her face.

"I'll talk," she told him. "I...I promise, I'll talk."

Looking at his partner with a grin, he said, "Alright, bitch, talk. Tell us what we want to hear. Tell us where the fuck Luke keeps all that bread."

With pain and torment evident in her voice, she told him, "The...the...the next time...I'm..."

Both men listened carefully.

"The next time...I'm...I'm on my period, eat my bloody pussy, bitch ass nigga. How's that? Is that what your soft ass wanted to hear?" She then laughed wildly. Her ribs ached terribly. But she forced the laughter.

Growing infuriated, the goon punched her twice. "You think this is a game, bitch? You think we're playing?" He pulled his gun out and prepared to pistol whip her until his partner stopped him.

Instead...More punches.

After several minutes, he said, "Alright, I've got something for you." He then pulled a pair of pliers from his back pocket.

Nessa weakly raised her throbbing head to see them.

"Let's see if this gets you to talk."

The man then latched the mouth of the pliers to the nail of Nessa's forefinger and began to pull until it ripped from its roots.

Nessa screamed at the top of her lungs in pain. Tears flowed from her eyes as she breathed heavily.

"Talk, bitch!"

She formed an even more stern face yet stayed silent as the tears continued to flow.

Another nail was ripped from her hand. She screamed even louder than before. The pain was unbearable. She'd never felt anything so excruciating.

"Where the fucking money at? Just tell us about one stash house and we'll let you live."

"Fuck you, muthafucka. Kill me!" she shouted.

Another slap.

Another punch.

"Kill me," she screamed. "Kill me, muthafuckas. And after you do, kill yourselves. Because when Luke finds out what you've done there won't be a place on earth your scum ass will be able to hide!"

With an open hand she was smacked viciously and knocked to the ground.

The slap brought Nessa back to current reality…still in the dark, creepy woods. The men now had her between them as they stood at what looked like a freshly dug grave. She was too weak to raise her head and didn't want to open her useable eye.

"Pay attention, bitch," the gunman who'd slapped her ordered. "This is the good part. You don't want to miss your own damn funeral, do you?"

From over the pit, Nessa looked down into it to see an opened casket sitting at the bottom. Inside the casket was a body covered in blood. Its eyes were open and staring directly up at her. Nessa immediately panicked.

Feeling and sensing her fear, both men laughed.

"Don't worry 'bout him, baby girl," one of them said. "We just put his ass in there to keep you company. He ain't gon' bite. He dead already."

They laughed again.

"Alright, bitch, last chance," she was told. "You want to tell us where those stash houses are? That's all it takes. Tell us what we want; we let you go 'bout your business."

Silently, Nessa saw Luke's face in her head. She heard his voice. All his motivational words…his loving words. She felt his kisses. She remembered the first time they met. She remembered their love making. She knew exactly where he kept most of his money and where his major stash houses were located. She could easily reveal the details and live. But each thought and memory made her tell her captors one final time…

"Fuck you."

She refused to turn on her man.

Shaking their heads, both men said almost at the exact same time, "Suit yourself then. You's a dead bitch, now."

With those words said, she was shoved into the pit and into the casket. Her body crashed down on the chest of the dead man as she screamed loudly.

"Noooooooooooo! Fuck Nooooooo! Don't do thisssssssss!"

She and he were now eye to eye. Her insides shook and bile rose up in her gut.

The casket shut.

Nessa vomited once again.

Darkness dominated.

Nessa, although hardened by the many things she'd experienced in life, broke down. She'd been taught to survive through several foster homes, abduction, family deaths, and violence at the hand of an old love, but nothing to this extreme. She couldn't help sobbing as she heard the dirt crashing down on the roof of the casket. Knowing she was going to be buried alive had her body shaking and her heart pounding.

As moment after moment passed by, she thought about Luke. She was dying inside knowing she'd never see him again. She wished she could tell him she loved him one last time. She wished she could kiss him one more time. She wished he had come to his senses and agreed to marry her before now.

More dirt crashed down.

Seconds seemed like hours.

Besides the vomit, the blood of the dead man underneath her turned her stomach. She could smell it. In fact, it wasn't a *smell*. It was a stench. It sickened her terribly. She wanted to cover her nostrils but her arms were far too weak. She could only lay there.

And wait to die.

A slow death.

Moments passed.

More dirt crashing down sounded.

More moments passed.

Suddenly…

Silence.

Nessa wondered why the sound of falling dirt had ceased. She listened closely. She could hear voices but couldn't make out what they were saying.

Then more silence.

Then…

The casket opened.

A shot gun was now in sight.

Moonlight immediately flooded the pit. Nessa, still in the most pain she'd ever experienced in her life, mustered up the strength to raise her head from the dead man's chest. Slightly, she turned to look toward the top of the pit. What she saw staring down at her both frightened and confused her...

Those eyes.

Those green eyes.

Was it really him?

CHAPTER 2

The tinted black S550 Mercedes Benz gracefully
slithered through D.C. a little after one a.m. Underneath
the night's full moon and glistening stars, the luxury whip
passed by war-torn, battered-beyond-repair
neighborhoods. Vacant buildings, lots and store fronts
lined main streets. Abandoned houses, unkempt lawns,
and busted out streetlamps lined side streets. The
neighborhoods were a far cry from the city's bustling and
brightly lit downtown. The west side seemed like the land
that time forgot.

Despite the time of night, the neighborhood's worst of
the worst and most disappointing roamed its streets and
sidewalks. Crackheads and prostitutes walked the shadows
on missions to find money to feed their drug habits. Their
faces and bodies showed the ravaging consequences of
years of addiction and abuse. Dope boys, most young and
strapped with guns, stood on corners anxious to sell them
the poison they chased endlessly day and night. From
distances not too far away gunshots echoed along with
blaring police sirens.

From the back seat of the Benz and from behind the darkness of the windows' tint, Luke stared out at the ghetto's hopeless and violent landscape in thought, knowing he was a huge reason why the entire city's black community had fallen into such turmoil. It was mainly the Heroin from his family's multimillion dollar Cocaine and Meth drug ring that flowed through their veins. It was his family's crack and marijuana that flooded their lungs. It was his family's guns that countless gangsters, including children, clutched while playing their part in running up the city's overwhelming murder rate.

Luke's family was undoubtedly the most successful family of kingpins Washington D.C. had seen since Rayful Edmonds. They hadn't achieved their success through only violence, intimidation and murder though. They'd also achieved it by building relationships and alliances with folks in high places. They had a man in the DEA. They had police officers on the take. They had a judge in their pocket. They were even due a few favors from the city's mayor because they had been a huge reason why the mayor won the election in the first place. During Mayor Walberg's campaign and electoral race, their family threatened and bullied voters into voting for him. The family also contributed thousands of dollars to the mayor's campaign. The assistance and influence resulted in a landslide win.

As Luke stared out of the car's window at the world around him, he felt more like a prisoner of his family's success than anything else. He felt more like a failure than an accomplished business man.

He felt like a criminal.

Somehow he hated the wealthy life and the past that led him to his current position. His family held so many secrets that most would puke, cry, and run for the hills if they got wind of what was taking place. Luke dropped his head and looked down at Nessa's battered and bruised face as it lay in his lap. Her eyes were closed. He grimaced at the sight as he began to rub her head softly. His eyes slowly roamed from her face down the entire length of her body. He saw bruises, cuts and blood. His nostrils smelled the stench of the blood and urine. He was sickened but not by what he saw. No; what sickened him was the part he himself had played in her assault.

Luke had given the order.

It nearly destroyed Luke when he ordered his goons to test the loyalty of the woman he loved. Nessa was his lady, his ride or die, his bitch; his number one. It shattered his heart in countless pieces to have to give such an order. But just like so many other things he despised during his life in this business, it had to be done. He had no choice but to accept it and hope she would still love him afterward. He had to be sure Nessa wasn't the insider feeding information to those after him.

Against his brother's fears, Luke had begun sharing private information about the family business over the last few months. He'd told her where he kept large sums of cash. She knew about a few of the stash houses. She knew workers, lawyers, contacts, and most of all, family secrets. Looking down at Nessa, Luke realized he'd made a good decision by trusting her.

The Mercedes turned off of a main street and into a dark alley. As the car's tires made their way down the alley's trash cluttered pavement, its headlight's brought into view a parked Cadillac Escalade. Two men were sitting inside; one in the driver's seat, the other in the passenger seat. Both goons had been the two who had inflicted Nessa's torture on her. After they dumped her in the makeshift grave, Luke sent them to handle crew business and then meet him here.

The brakes of the Benz's factory rimmed wheels squealed lightly as the car came to an abrupt stop. After placing the whip in park, the driver stepped out and began to make his way along the passenger side towards the trunk and around to Luke's door. When he reached the door, he opened it graciously.

Luke eased his thigh from underneath Nessa's head and replaced it with the palm of his hand as he slid out of the backseat. With his hand he lovingly rested her head down on the seat. He then took off his suit jacket revealing a shoulder holster and gun. His once white dress shirt was now stained in Nessa's blood. The thighs of his pants were also. He softly placed the suit coat over her. A moment later he slipped his hands into a pair of plastic gloves.

Nessa, still dazed from her beating, mumbled something incoherently to Luke. "Shhhhhhh," he said, placing his lips to her ear softly. "I'll be back shortly. I promise." He then kissed her on the cheek affectionately and shut the door.

Stuffing his hands into the pockets of his pants, Luke and his driver headed towards the Escalade. Behind them, The Mercedes's headlights shined illuminating the area between them and the SUV. As they walked, the heels of Luke's fourteen hundred dollar, Tom Ford loafers clicked and echoed off the walls of the abandoned buildings lining both sides of the narrow alleyway. The two men awaiting them in the SUV climbed out. Both groups of men met up in front of the Escalade's hood.

"The two of you did an exceptional job tonight," Luke commended them while still keeping his hands in his pockets. "You do good work."

Both goons looked at each other and smiled proudly, glad that their work was to their bossman's liking. Everyone wanted to please Luke at all times, no matter the cost.

"I appreciate that," Luke told them.

"It was nothin'," one of the men replied. "Whatever you need done, you know we're always game for that shit."

"Really?" Luke asked, glaring at the huge gap between his teeth.

"That's right, boss."

"Even if I ordered you to smoke our boy here?"

The man turned to his partner with a sinister stare. Then looked back at Luke.

The moment became far too weird.

"It's all business, right?" he asked Luke then shrugged his shoulders.

Luke nodded. He then looked at his driver and said, "Pay these soldiers. They've done what I asked."

The driver reached into his suit jacket's inner pocket, pulled out an envelope and handed it to one of the goons. The goon didn't even bother to open it. With a smile on his face, he simply stuffed it in the front pocket of his jeans.

"You're not going to count it?" Luke asked.

"Nahhhh, you're good. We trust you."

"Important rule, gentlemen; never trust anyone."

The goons nodded.

With that said, Luke turned to head back to the Benz. His driver did also. After taking several steps, Luke stopped, turned and said as if he'd forgotten something, "Oh, gentlemen, one other thing?"

The two goons were heading around the hood of the Escalade as he spoke. They stopped and turned to him. "What's up, boss?"

Luke pulled his hands from his pockets, grabbed the gun from his holster, took aim at the man on the truck's driver side and squeezed the trigger.

Amidst the gun's thundering blast, its bullet tore through the man's forehead and ripped the entire back of his skull off. Brain, skull and patches of hair scattered on the ground and the Escalade's driver's side door. The man crumpled to the ground.

"What the fuck?" the man on the passenger side said in surprise and disbelief. Fear quickly captured his entire face as his eyes went from where his partner was once standing to Luke.

Luke immediately took aim at him. With one last glare into the gap between his teeth he sighed. "Respect is everything."

Raising his hands in defense, his eyes wide, the goon asked, "What did I do?"

Without giving him an answer, Luke squeezed the trigger again. The back of the man's head exploded just like his partner's had done. He hit the ground a second later. Luke then walked over to the first man and stood over him. Blood spilled from the back of his skull and flowed endlessly. Luke, unfazed by the blood, let off three shots in the man's chest to insure he was dead. As he did, each shot was accompanied by bright flashes from the gun. Empty shell casings spilled from the side of the barrel onto the ground. Immediately after the last shot was fired, he headed around the hood to the second man. Seeing him lying on his back with half his head gone and his legs twitching, Luke fired three shots into his chest. The man's body went totally still.

Silence.

Brief moments passed.

Luke turned and walked back to his driver. The driver didn't say anything. He'd seen countless men murdered in this business, the game his employer was in. This one wasn't expected though. There had been no forewarning. Instead of saying a word though, he only looked at Luke with a sort of bewildered stare. Knowing what the driver wanted to ask, Luke said to him, "No man should know how it feels to harm another man's woman and live."

With those words said, Luke handed the handle of the gun to the driver and said, "Get rid of the gun and the bodies. I'll drive myself home."

Taking off the rubber gloves, Luke headed to the Benz.

CHAPTER 3

The white stucco, three million dollar, two-storied mansion sat on 6.5 acres of breathtaking land in Potomac Maryland. It was surrounded by plush green lawns, a long circular drive way, a three-bedroom guest house, golf course, basketball court, and an Olympic sized swimming pool. Inside, it was laced with marble floors, towering high ceilings, eight bedrooms, six bathrooms, a movie theater, a butler, maid and so much more.

The Mercedes made its way up the cobble stone drive way and parked beneath the home's wide staircase. Luke shut off the car's engine and hopped out. Moments later, with Nessa in his arms, he made his way up the stairs toward the front door. Her head rested against his chest and her arms were wrapped around his shoulders as he walked. As he reached the top of the stairs, the home's fourteen foot French styled double doors opened. A man resembling Luke, only younger and with freshly done dreads appeared. He was dressed in a pair of Louis Vuitton high top sneakers, black Louis Vuitton jeans which sagged, and a white wife beater that revealed chiseled and exotically detailed tattoos from neck to shoulder. His name was Darien, Luke's little brother.

Stepping into the foyer, Luke asked his brother, "Are the doctor and nurse here yet?"

Darien looked at Nessa's battered body. "Yeah, they're in the main room."

"Good. Tell them to meet me upstairs in the master bedroom in ten minutes. I need a minute with her to myself."

Darien closed the door. "How'd she fend? I mean, is she ride or die, or nah?"

"She's everything I thought she was," Luke answered as he headed towards the sweeping staircase which was actually two separate staircases that curved towards each other as they rose and met at the top. In between them were a gorgeous fountain and a walkway that led to one of the house's two dens.

As Luke carried Nessa up the stairs, he noticed a striking woman standing at the second floor railing directly in the center of where the staircases met. Just like Darien, she bore resemblance to Luke, just older and feminine. Her name was Mrs. Bishop, Luke's mother, whom most called Chetti.

Chetti was a slim, Brazilian looking woman in her mid-fifties who carried herself more like a fiery woman in her thirties. Her long, naturally wavy hair, which hung to her elbows, had been dyed a bronze shade with bright blonde highlights, giving her the appearance of an islander. Her facial features, although obviously aged, still had an exotic look to them. Her brown eyes had a natural slant to them although there was no Asian blood anywhere in her family.

Holding a glass of expensive, imported Tequila, which she always drank straight; no chaser, Chetti was dressed in a black, lace embroidered La Perla night gown. Her pedicured feet were bare. The hair on the left side of her face purposely draped over her left eye and the entire left side of her face concealing it totally as she stared out over the first floor like a queen proudly surveying her empire.

Luke was nearly at the top of the stairs when his mother asked without looking at him, keeping her gaze over the railing, "What happened to her?" Her tone was cold, purposely designed to show she had no genuine concern for Nessa's current state. She'd never liked Nessa and wasn't going to start now.

Hearing the coldness in his mother's voice, Luke didn't answer her as he reached the top step.

Shrugging her shoulders and still gazing over the railing, she said, "Bitch probably deserved it. There's a reason why trash is best left in the streets." Her voice was filled with arrogance and privilege.

"Mother, don't speak on things you know nothing about," Luke told her as he passed behind her back.

Chetti's nostrils caught a strong whiff of the urine and blood radiating from Nessa's body when Luke walked by. Making a distasteful face, she said, "Even *smells* like trash." She took a sip of her Tequila and shook her head. Ice cubes clinked against the sides of the glass.

"Bitch," Nessa whispered with her face still resting against Luke's chest. Nessa hated Chetti just as much Chetti hated her.

Luke continued to ignore his mother as he made his way down the hall. Oddly, his mother had no idea how much Luke really disliked her. He respected and loved her, but detested her at the same time. When he reached the master bedroom and opened the door, from behind him she yelled, "I'll be sure to have the maid burn the sheets. Then I'll be sure to have her burn the fucking bed!"

Luke shut the door as his mother's arrogant laughter began to fill the hall. He carried Nessa across the marble floor of the huge bedroom and laid her softly on the silk sheets of the king-sized bed they shared most nights. Sitting beside her, he gazed at her beauty silently.

Moments passed before Luke finally spoke. "You know this had to be done, right?"

Nessa might've been badly battered and bruised, but her ability to comprehend was fully in tact. She knew exactly what he meant.

Nessa's eye, the one that wasn't swollen shut, opened and looked up at Luke as he began to get up from the bed. She grabbed his arm. "Why?" she whispered with the back of her head resting on the lavish pillow. A tear began to roll down the side of her face.

Suddenly, there was a knock at the door.

"Give me a moment!" he shouted to the door, knowing it was the doctor and nurse who'd been waiting on standby to treat Nessa. He looked back down at her.

"Why?" she asked again, her voice still just above a whisper. She felt betrayed and her saddened face showed it. "Why did you do this to me? I thought you loved me."

Looking her directly in the eyes, Luke told her in a tone just a low as her own, "I did it *because* I love you."

Nessa didn't understand. Not at all. In the past she'd always trusted anything Luke told her. He was seventeen years older than Nessa and a lot wiser. Whatever plans he had for them, Nessa normally went along with it.

"If I didn't love you, you would be dead," he said. "I had to be sure I could trust you."

Nessa peered into the pair of mesmerizing green eyes she loved so much.

"Haven't I proved that already? Isn't my word enough?"

"*Now* it is. But you know people were finding out things about me that no one should know."

"And so you thought it was me?" she asked hurtfully. The two fell silent.

A knock came from the door again.

"Come back in fifteen minutes!" Luke shouted.

Luke began to stroke the side of Nessa's face softly. "You're the most beautiful woman in this world to me," he said, truly meaning it. "Even your scars are beautiful."

"You mean that?"

The moment Luke grabbed a hold of Nessa's hands, guilt filled him again after seeing her finger's damaged nail beds. As usual, he felt like he needed to spoil Nessa. And in this case pay for torturing her.

Reaching into his pocket and pulling out several stacks, he said, "Here, take this for now. After the doctors fix you up nicely, I'm taking you to Paris. You're going to get everything you deserve and more."

Instantly, Nessa threw the stack of money to the side as if she didn't want it. She couldn't speak.

A tear fell.

Then another.

"You know what I want, Luke."

His eyes met hers as if there was some secret code between them.

Placing his face between her hands still covered in dried up blood, Luke heard Nessa say, "I need a shower then I want you to make love to me."

Luke kissed her softly. "No shower needed. I want you just the way you are."

He took off his empty shoulder holster, unbuttoned his blood stained shirt and threw it on the floor revealing a muscular chest and a six-pack laced stomach. He had no tattoos or scars. For a forty year old man, Luke was cut, especially in his upper body area.

Staring up into Luke's eyes, Nessa laid there as he undressed her delicately like an expensive doll. Knowing her body was fragile from the torture she'd suffered, he didn't want to hurt her. His compassion and thoughtfulness made her pussy wet. She wanted him inside her.

Luke, after getting Nessa undressed, began to kiss her lips. The taste of her blood didn't bother him at all. The stench of urine didn't turn his stomach. Whatever her pain or discomfort, he wanted to be a part of it. He wanted to join with her.

"I love you," she whispered into his ear as he began to plant gentle kisses around her neck.

"I love you, too," he whispered back.

"So, are you ready to marry me now?"

Luke's dick throbbed inside of his pants as he placed kisses all over her breasts. He didn't want to discuss marriage. He wanted to make love. He'd never wanted Nessa more than he wanted her right now. The feeling was intensifying.

"You hear me, Luke? I asked, are you ready to marry me now?"

Luke continued his foreplay session for several seconds before final telling Nessa, "Can we talk about this later? I want you, now."

Although her missing fingernails had her hands aching, Nessa bore the pain as she reached for the button of Luke's pants. She too had gotten extremely horny and wanted Luke inside of her. Quickly, Luke had taken off his clothes and watched as Nessa took hold of his dick, and began to stroke it.

"Ahhhhhhhh, baby," he moaned.

"You're everything in this world to me, Luke," she whispered into his ear.

"You too, baby girl," he returned.

Luke began to plant wet kisses on Nessa's stomach. As he did, he noticed the bruises on her belly, ribs and arms. He was face to face with them. Realizing Nessa had gone through the ultimate sacrifice for him and succeeded, he began licking her thighs and kissing her bruises. Nessa's right thigh was special to Luke. It was the leg that showcased the tattoo of his name, along with Nessa's choice of flowers and tiger paws.

"I love you so much, baby," Nessa whispered as she closed her eyes and basked in her man's kisses.

Luke worked his way down to Nessa's pussy, a place he visited often. He sucked her clit softly and gently causing it to swell and harden. He then placed her thighs over his shoulders, slipped his tongue inside the pussy and began to work it deeply.

"Oh Luke," she whispered as she grabbed onto his bald head.

Luke worked the pussy with his tongue even more vigorously. The taste was driving him crazy. He needed all of it. He had to *have* all of it. Getting a tighter grip on Nessa's thighs, he buried his face in her box as far as he could and began to lap out her tunnel so savagely his mouth made loud slurping sounds.

"Babyyyyy," she moaned as she arched her back up from the bed. Her toes curled. Her hands and fingers got a tighter grip on his skull. Her body still ached from the torture she'd endured earlier but the pleasure Luke was giving her seemed to drown it out.

Luke continued feasting.

Moments passed.

Suddenly…

A loud knock at the door.

"I'll tell you when I'm ready for you!" Luke yelled back, figuring it was the doctor and nurse again.

Darien's voice came from behind the door. "It's me, nigga. It's important!"

Luke reluctantly climbed off of Nessa, threw on his pants and walked across the room to the door. Opening it, but using himself to block Nessa's naked body, he could tell by the look on his brother's face and the growing rage in his eyes something was wrong. "What is it?" he asked.

"It's bad," Darien told him with a silver chromed glock in his hand. He'd pulled his dreads into a tight ponytail. "It's *real* fuckin' bad. We gotta go right now."

"Alright." Luke shut the door, grabbed his shirt and kissed Nessa. "I'll be back as soon as I can," he told her.

"Nooooo, Luke. Not now."

"Nessa, look, some people have been after me for a while. This is serious. Stay here. You'll be safe." Seconds later, he was gone.

Nessa lay on her back in a daze. Without Luke there to pleasure her, the pain of the beating and torture she took came back. It began to make her wince.

"Damn humanitarian project," Chetti said, leaning against the frame of the door looking at Nessa. She was still holding her glass of Tequila.

"What?" Nessa asked, pulling the sheets over her naked body.

"You're a humanitarian project for my son, a mercy fuck even. Just something to stick his dick in until the next one comes along."

"You know what, Chetti maybe that's what *your* damn problem is. Maybe you need some good dick

178

shoved in that decrepit cobweb infested pussy of yours. Maybe if you got a mercy fuck or whatever kind of fuck, you'd be less of a bitch."

Chetti chuckled.

The two women went back and forth like this often, mainly behind Luke's back.

"You know what else I think your problem is?" Nessa asked.

"No, ghetto trash, enlighten me. Or better yet, crackbaby, *humor* me."

"You know that I'm more than just the latest bitch in Luke's long line of conquests. You see it in his eyes every time he looks at me. You hear it in his voice every time he talks *to* me or *about* me."

Chetti smirked.

"And you especially hear it in his moans when you're listening outside the door, which I know you do often with your sneaky ass. You hear him all up inside my pussy, don't you?"

Chetti's eyes narrowed.

Knowing she had gotten to Chetti, Nessa went further. She smiled and said, "It eats your miserable ass up inside to know that I'm next in line for *your* job. I'm next in line to be the queen of this family. And know that I'll be spending the millions that your husband left to you and your sons. As soon as they throw the dirt on your boney, decrepit, and dried up lookin' ass, I'll be calling the shots around here. Shit, I'm only twenty-three, I've got time to watch you die."

Unable to keep her composure, Chetti slammed her glass to the floor so hard it shattered. "Let me tell you something, you weave having video vixen reject," she said with fury in her eyes and face. "I've been running this family alongside my husband ever since your parents were standing in line during the Reagan era for government cheese. I've brokered more business deals than you can count. I've sent more motherfuckers to the poorhouse than the IRS. I've lunched with countless fashion designers in Paris while the closest *you've* ever gotten to them is wearing that cheap-ass True Religion."

Nessa eyed her closely. She'd never seen her so furious.

"But most importantly, bitch, and pay attention because this is the part that really pertains directly to you,"

Chetti told her with a cold glare. "I've had more motherfuckers killed than The Vietnam War. I'm as lethal as poison. The fucking AIDS virus ain't got shit on me."

Nessa didn't speak. She knew the grimace on Luke's mother's face meant something wicked. Luke had shared with her some vicious things his mother had done to her enemies in the past. She wasn't to be fucked with.

"So if you've got eyes on my spot, hoe," Chetti continued, "I suggest you pick out a cemetery plot because I will personally be there to witness one of my goons put a bullet through the center of your head before I allow that. It's only because of the love I have for my son that you're alive this long or even living in this house. Don't get it twisted. I may be older than you but pushing your luck can be fatal when dealing with a bitch like me."

Suddenly, the doctor and nurse walked into the bedroom unannounced. Looking at them and smiling, Chetti said, "Get her fixed up very nicely. There's a tip in it for you. I want her to look just as good as new when she takes her one way trip back to the ghetto." She looked at Nessa and winked. A moment later, she was gone.

As the doctor and nurse began to tend to Nessa's wounds, the look on her face was a cold one as she kept her eyes locked on the spot where her new enemy had been standing. The old bitch had pissed her off countless times. They'd teed off more times than either of them could count. The little disagreements had never gotten to Nessa. This time though, it was different. It *had* gotten to her. Nessa was far beyond pissed off. Chetti had threatened her life with intentions of scaring her off. Little did she know though her threat had birthed something relentless inside Nessa. Now as Nessa lay there in bed, she promised herself she was going to be the queen of the Bishop family no matter what it took.

CHAPTER 4

The engine of the yellow Aston Martin Vanquish with black trim growled menacingly as its tires sharply turned to the right causing it to whip up into the dark parking lot. As it headed toward the old abandoned bread factory in Northwest D.C., its headlights brought several parked SUVs into view, each of them parked side by side. Several men holding guns stood among them.

Gravel spurted from underneath the Aston Martin's tires as it headed directly toward the line of SUV's. Seconds later, it screeched to a halt. Quickly both its doors swung open. Darien hopped out of the driver's side while Luke emerged from the passenger side.

Approaching them, one of the awaiting gunmen said to them as they met up in front of the Aston Martin, "It's real fucked up in there." He shook his head as he spoke. "Some real live horror movie type shit."

Anger was all over Darien's face. His eyes were bloodshot with something far beyond rage. Darien definitely wasn't the type who took situations like this well and with a grain of salt. Luke on the other hand, was calm. The expression on his face showed no hint whatsoever of what he felt or thought. He never showed emotion, no matter the situation. Luke's motto was "Wise men think when super composed".

Pissed off, ignoring his soldier, Darien brushed passed him bumping his shoulder with such force he knocked him out of the way. He immediately headed for the factory with his eyes locked on its entrance. Nothing around him was worth even a morsel of interest at that moment. Luke and the rest of the soldiers followed behind him.

The factory was empty. The rows of wall to wall equipment that once filled the room had been removed shortly after it was shut down. It now smelled of mildew, urine, feces, and Lord knows whatever as the men entered inside. Decades worth of garbage littered the floors. Grime and mud soiled them also as syringes, discarded condoms, beer cans, shattered wine bottles and much more were scattered about. The walls were covered in graffiti.

"Where they at?" Darien asked as he now stood inside the factory with a heavy scowl on his face.

"Upstairs," a gunman told him.

Everyone headed up a set of iron stairs to the second floor. The soles of their shoes and boots echoed against the walls. As soon as they reached the top, death bombarded their nostrils. Dairen and Luke could actually smell the stench of blood. There was no mistaking it. They'd killed enough men to know exactly how it smelled. Right now its stench was thick and heavy. Its nauseating smell though was nothing compared to the sight awaiting them.

Darien froze.

Luke stood beside his brother.

Their eyes stared at the mayhem and bloodshed in front of them.

As moonlight shined into the second floor through the frames' broken windows, several men were scattered about the floor dead. They weren't just dead though; they were posed in humiliating and degrading positions. One of them was bent at the waist over a table with his arms outstretched. Nails had been driven into the backs of his hands through his palms to pin him to the table. His jeans and boxers were pulled down around his ankles. A broken broom stick had been shoved into his rectum; the broken end first.

Another man hung from the rafters by his neck. A rope was tied around his neck. His body was completely naked. His hands were tied behind his back. His eyes, although lifeless, were wide open as they stared off into the distance ahead of him while his head leaned limply across his left shoulder. There were no bullet wounds and no blood dripping from his body so it was safe to assume he'd been hung up there while he was alive.

All together there were nine men scattered about the room. All were dead. The factory was a meeting point where a transaction involving fifteen kilos was supposed to take place. Obviously the men had been ambushed, robbed, and a whole lot worse.

Luke made his way to the man bent over the table. When he reached him, he stared at him for a moment. The side of the dead man's head lay flat on the table with his eyes open. Those eyes were now staring directly into Luke's. Luke didn't say a word. He just let his own eyes begin to survey the long knife inflicted gash that ran across the man's throat from his right ear to his left. Blood was spilling from it to the table. It was pooling underneath the man's upper body and dripping heavily to the floor gathering in a small pool that was gradually spreading.

"Muthafuckas!" Darien yelled angrily as he walked across the floor surveying the damage. "Muthafuckin' cock suckers!"

Luke didn't let his eyes or attention leave the man on the table. He recognized him. That said a lot. The family's organization, especially its gunmen, runners and all those who did the dirty work, was a huge one. There were countless faces, some went just as quickly as they came and they were all expendable. *This* one though, Luke remembered. The man was in his early twenties. He'd seen Luke out somewhere and asked him for a job personally. He'd said he had been out of the penitentiary for several months and wasn't having any luck finding a job. He'd also said his fiancé was expecting their first child. Not truly giving him a second look, Luke simply gave him a number to a low level associate and kept it moving. Now though, Luke was definitely giving the man a second look.

Luke found himself bothered at the moment. He realized he didn't even know this man's name, a man who worked for him, a man whose job it was to place his freedom and life on the line for him. But the realization that gripped Luke the most was knowing that crossing paths with this man had cost him his life. It had cost a child their father. Allowing his hand to swipe his bald head, he joined his brother's rant about retaliation.

"Them sons of bitches gon' pay for this shit!" Luke yelled. He was beyond pissed off. "I swear they gon' pay!"

Luke finally walked away from the dead man who'd just captivated his thoughts. His face though and the gash across his throat was etched inside Luke's head.

Beginning to survey each man, Luke walked over them stepping in their blood and leaving a trail of bloody shoe prints behind himself. As his eyes took in everything, the sight was nothing new to him. It wasn't like he hadn't seen stuff like this before. He'd seen it countless times. It was a part of the business. This time though, it seemed different. It felt different.

Just like in the car watching over the battered body of the woman he loved, Luke was now second guessing his life and his profession. He'd been doing that a lot lately. The game had never bothered him up until the past few months. He didn't quite know why. He just knew he was developing a conscience. He was developing compassion. He was becoming something neither the game nor his own father had raised him to be...

Civilized.

Mr. Bishop had raised his sons in the underworld. He'd taught them to kill and how to become wealthy no matter the circumstance. He'd taught them the menacing ropes of running a crime family, especially during their teenage years. Yet most had no idea of some of the values he'd instilled in them that Luke was totally against then and now.

Luckily for Luke, after his death, he passed the reins over to them and their mother, allowing Luke more freedom to stray away from some of the disturbing ways their father truly believed in. Luke had been proud at that moment to carry on the family legacy. He'd been proud to finally play a part in expanding the family business. These days though, that feeling was fading.

As Luke now approached a young man lying on the floor, the first thing he noticed was that the young man's pants were down and he was clutching his crotch. Blood spilled from underneath his hands. As Luke neared him, he saw that the man's body seemed to be trembling.

He was still alive.

Luke rushed to him. When he reached him though, his heart sunk to his stomach. Just like the man bent over the table, Luke recognized this man, or rather this young boy. He was only seventeen. His name was Gavin.

He was Luke and Darien's nephew.

The two brothers had a sister named Trinity. She'd walked away from the family long ago, not wanting any parts of its bloody legacy or its crooked business dealings. She'd even gone as far as to change her last name. The last time the two brothers and even their mother saw her was at their dad's funeral, four years ago.

Gavin, although forbidden by his mother to even associate with his uncles, eventually got in touch with Darien. He'd heard the stories in the streets of how ruthless and respected the family was. He wanted to be a part of it. He wanted to be a gangster just like the rappers he'd heard and seen in countless videos on BET but could never get a crew to take him seriously because of his slight deformity. Sadly, Gavin was born with muscular dystrophy but never allowed it to keep him from engaging in the activities he yearned; a life of crime mostly. Since his early teen years he'd kept in touch with his uncles, uncles who loved him dearly. So of course when the time came, Darien, behind Trinity's back and against Luke's wishes, gave him a job.

Now he was nearly dead.

Luke rushed to his nephew's aid. Gurgling and choking, Gavin lay on the floor with his own dick shoved deeply into his mouth. Blood oozed from several bullet wounds in his stomach and chest. Ripping the penis from his nephew's mouth and tossing it, Luke quickly knelt and took his nephew's head into his arms. "Darien!" he screamed.

"I...I...can't..." Gavin attempted as blood ran from his mouth down the sides of his face onto Luke's lap. His eyes were wide. His chest was heaving up and down underneath his T-shirt quickly.

"Darien!" Luke called again as he sat underneath his nephew's head holding him in his arms. His eyes quickly darted up and down at his wounds taking in the bullet holes and pouring crimson liquid. He was almost in shock himself at the sight.

Darien rushed towards them. When he reached them, recognizing his nephew, his eyes grew wide. He shook his head in disbelief.

"Nooooooo!" Darien hollered, refusing to accept what he was seeing. "No," he said again. He just kept repeating that word over and over. "It can't be." He began pacing the floor while looking at his nephew. "Fuck!" he yelled. "Them muthafuckas gon' pay!" he shouted while throwing a metal object into a pole.

Luke began to rock back and forth while cradling his nephew's head. "You're gonna be alright, Gavin," he said knowing it wasn't true. He just hoped his words could somehow help Gavin through the moment. "We're gonna get you fixed up."

Looking up into his uncle's eyes, Gavin whispered, "I...I...can't feel...my...my...legs."

"You're gonna be okay," Luke assured him again.

"I can't...feel...feel them...Uncle...Uncle Luke."

Terror, pain, sadness, bewilderment and so many other expressions were on Gavin's young face as his eyes stayed locked on his Uncle's face. His body shook uncontrollably. "They...did...did... me bad."

"Don't speak, Gavin," Luke told him. "It's going to be okay. You're going to be back on your feet in no time."

"Unc, they... wanna... kill...you."

"Shhh," Luke told him.

Then...

Luke wasn't prepared for Gavin's next set of words...

"Kill me," Gavin said.

Luke stared at his nephew, not sure if his ears were playing tricks on him. He was sure he hadn't heard his nephew correctly. He couldn't have.

"Kill...kill...kill me, Uncle Luke."

Luke realized he *had* heard him correctly. Hearing them the second time hit him like a brick. He didn't even know how to respond.

"Please…please…Uncle Luke…kill kill me."

Shaking his head, Luke said, "Stop talking like that."

"Look at me, Unc. Look…look at…at me. Look… at what they…did to me."

He coughed up blood. A moment later he began to cough up his insides. He gritted his teeth at the pain. Tears began to fall from the outer corners of his eyes and roll down the sides of his face.

Darien had stopped pacing. He was now standing silently and staring down at his nephew.

Continuing on, Gavin said, "They cut my manhood off, man." Hurt and shame on his face. He began to cry even worse than before. Amidst his tears, he said, "They cut my- f-u-c-k-i-n dick off." He hesitated then continued, "I can't live like that."

Luke looked up at Darien who'd he'd never seen shed a tear in life. He was now glossy-eyed. Neither brother spoke. Their eyes just glared into each other's. Luke then looked back down at his nephew.

"Unc, I can't feel my legs," Gavin told him. "They took my dick. I can't go through fucking life like this."

Luke squeezed his nephew's hand tightly.

"Kill me," Gavin begged. "Please don't make me suffer."

The gunmen had now gathered. They stood around their two generals as they watched their own flesh and blood beg to die. They all stood silent.

"Kill me, Uncle Luke," Gavin whispered with more tears falling from his eyes. "Shoot me. Allow me some type of honor."

"Shhhhhhhh," Luke told him as he placed his index finger to his own lips.

Gavin didn't say another word. He just continued to stare up at his uncle hoping he'd grant his wish. His body continued to tremble. His heart beat thumped loudly. The pain of the gunshots and his castration was growing more and more unbearable. He looked like a scared little boy; a little boy who hadn't been terrorizing the streets of D.C. just days before.

Luke placed his thumb and index finger over his nephew's eyes and shut them. He then softly kissed him on the forehead, savoring its taste on his lips for as long as he could. Slowly he slid out from underneath him while laying the back of his head softly on the floor. Now standing and looking his brother in the eyes, he extended his hand for his gun. Darien obliged him. He placed the gun in his brother's hand. Luke then looked down brokenheartedly at his dying nephew. As he did, he remembered the day Trinity had proudly told him she was pregnant. He remembered being at her side in the delivery room as she gave birth. He remembered holding Gavin in his arms for the very first time. Each of those moments tormented him.

Luke aimed the gun and cocked the slide of the barrel.

No one said a word.

All eyes were on Gavin.

Moments passed.

Finally…

CRACK!!!

CRACK!!!

CRACK!!!

Luke squeezed the trigger letting off three shots into his nephew's chest. Within a brief second, Gavin's breathing stopped and his body went completely still. A louder and more intense silence than before seemed to fall over the room. With no hesitation Luke gave the gun back to his brother and walked off.

"Wait 'till mom hears about this shit," Darien said following his brother. "Blood is finna run all over these muthafuckin' streets. We're gonna kill all those niggas."

Luke ignored Darien. He headed down the stairs to the first floor.

"What do you think? Do you think we should hit their asses tonight, bruh?"

Luke didn't say a word. He headed out the door.

"Luke!"

Luke continued walking. He even walked right past Darien's car.

"Luke, what's up? Where you goin'?"

Luke turned to his brother. Looking him directly in the eyes, he said, "We're getting out of this game."

Dairen looked at him like he was crazy. "What?"

"We're getting out, Darien."

"What the fuck you mean?"

"We're exiting this business as soon as possible; the guns, drugs, prostitution, everything; all of it. We're getting out."

Darien was pissed. "What the fuck you mean? Nigga, you trippin'. That's our nephew in there."

"You're muthafuckin' right that's our nephew!!!!!" Luke roared back at his brother louder than Darien had ever heard him yell before. Luke rarely yelled. He never showed emotion. He never even cursed. This was a surprise to Darien.

"I just had to kill our sister's only child, Darien!" Luke continued. "We just lost nine men. And that's just *tonight*. That doesn't include the men we've lost over the *years*!"

Darien didn't speak.

"Eventually one of those men are going to be *us*, Darien. One of these days it's going to be *us* lying on the floor with a bullet in our heads!"

"Then that's chance we have to take, Luke. When we took over the business the day dad died, that's what we signed the fuck on for!"

Luke shook his head, angry that his brother wasn't seeing things the way he was.

"*We're* the nightmares, Luke!" Darien shouted. "*We're* the boogiemen. We make *other* muthafuckas retire from the game. *We* do that. Since when the fuck did that shit get twisted?"

"Fuck that! Darien, we're getting the fuck out of this game. There are too many other opportunities out there for us to find success in. And most of them are legal. We're going to take advantage of them!"

"Sounds like a coward move to me. I mean think about it. You got niggas in these streets after you. Instead of takin' care of them you wanna run like a lil' bitch!"

Losing his cool, Luke charged his brother, snatched him by the collar of his wife beater and forced him backwards towards the Aston Martin. Slamming him onto the hood so hard the entire car rocked, he said angrily and through gritted teeth, "Don't you ever in your muthafuckin' life call me a coward again!"

Darien didn't say anything. From the hood of the car, he didn't quite know what to make of his brother. He'd never seen his brother like this before. He'd never seen him that furious.

Luke finally let go of his brother. Taking a step back and calming himself, he said in a calmer tone than before,

"Those men in there had families. They had people who loved them, Darien."

"They knew that comin' into this shit, Luke. You can't pick and choose what days you wanna be a gangsta. You either in or out." Darien shrugged his shoulders nonchalantly.

"It doesn't have to be this way, Darien. I mean this game is like a revolving door, a never ending cycle. They kill us. We kill them. They make a move on us. We make a move on them. They lose men. We lose men. When the fuck does it stop, Darien?"

Darien didn't answer.

"We retaliate, they're going to retaliate. And eventually you and me are going to be caught in the cross fire, little brother."

"That's just the way it is," Darien told him shrugging it off. "To whom much is given, much is required. Ain't that what you always say?"

Luke sighed. He knew there was no getting through to Darien. Shaking his head, he turned around and headed off into the night.

"Where you goin'?" Darien shouted to him.

"For a walk!" Luke shouted over his shoulder.

"How you gon' get home?"

No answer.

"It's dangerous out there, nigga. Did you forget some very dangerous people want you dead?" he shouted.

Still no answer.

Darien said to a nearby soldier, "Follow him." Despite he and his brother's confrontation and difference of opinion, Darien still needed to be sure his brother was safe.

Dear Diary

Things getting real crazy. It's hard to trust anybody these days; especially bitches. First she told me she'd handle things then she told me to wait a little longer…now the bitch is ignoring my calls.

One fact is for sure. I never had a problem murking a muthafucka. Shit's about to get REAL.

CHAPTER 5

The leather seats of the brand new white Bentley Wrath were unique leather and super soft. The dark tint of the windows casted a dark shadow over the entire interior. The dashboard's digital array of speedometers, stereo system, gave off a bluish glow, and the engine growled loudly each time Nessa's nude Giuseppe Zanotti pump pressed down on the gas pedal even in the least.

Dressed casually in a long, fashionable Helmut Lang tee, ripped jeans and Chanel sunglasses that hid her black eyes, Nessa leaned back into the driver's seat of the three hundred thousand dollar car as its air conditioning blew cool air from the dashboard vents. Her eyes were on the sunny highway ahead of her, but her mind wasn't. It was in deep thought and worry.

Sitting beside Nessa was her home-girl, Sidra. The two had been friends since their freshman year at Anacostia Senior High School. They'd been inseparable ever since.

"You alright?" Sidra asked.

Nessa didn't answer as the speeding cars on Suitland Parkway passed by her window. Nessa even found herself taking quick glances of the ocean blue sky. It was a beautiful summer day. She hadn't even heard her friend. Her mind was too focused on locating Luke.

"Nessa!" Sidra called out.

"What's up?" Nessa finally responded.

"I don't know. You tell me. I've been over here running my mouth like a dog race to your ass for the past fifteen minutes and you haven't said a damn word. You haven't even looked at me. What's going on?"

Nessa shook her head and told her, "Sorry, girl. Just got my mind on a lot of shit right now."

"Like what?"

"Just stuff."

Sidra nodded then twisted her lips into a nasty funk. "It's Luke, right?"

Nessa simply shook her head.

"Men do that shit to you. All of them fuckas."

"Being with him is starting to stress me the fuck out."

Looking at her friend like she'd lost her mind, Sidra asked, "Stressing you? Bitch, are you crazy? What the fuck do you have to be stressed about?"

"A lot. I can't…" Nessa paused to choose her words wisely. She knew the rules of the Bishop family. No one could be trusted and no one needed to know even the tiniest detail about their personal business.

"What? Say it…" Sidra urged.

"It's nothing. Just forget about it."

Nessa chuckled at her friend's crazy looking facial expression.

"Bitch, you livin' in a mansion out in Potomac, Maryland while most of the niggas I fuck wit' ain't never been out of Southeast. You drive the baddest fuckin' whip in town, and got a slew of choices in Luke's six car garage. Andddddddd…you're rockin' the baddest shoes and clothes."

Nessa's mind refocused. She thought of her designer wardrobe. The one filled with clothes that every girl wanted to have and the one with countless pairs of Louboutins, Valentino's and Gucci's. Not to mention, her handbag collection would even make a basketball wife jealous. From Celine, Louis Vuitton to YSL and Hermes…Nessa had it all.

"Shiiittt…your ass always look good. I gained at least fifteen pounds since the last time I've seen you," Sidra added. "I mean do you remember how fine I was in high school? I used to have a bad ass body like Kim Kardashian." Sidra quickly looked into the sun visor's mirror. "And I gotta get this ratchet-ass weave done, too," she said, studying her ombre colored weave. "I need a total fuckin' makeover."

Sidra's rambling brought Nessa back to reality. "And let me add, you have one of the finest niggas in the DMV area. Bitch please, what the hell are you trippin' about? Work the game. Don't let the game work you."

Nessa shrugged her shoulders and took a hand off the wheel to push her sunglasses further onto her face.

Looking out of her own window, Sidra added, "That's a long way from the damn Barry Farm, boo boo I'll tell you that. You came up. You found a way out. Don't let the small shit get to you."

Nessa thought deeply about her friend's words. Secretly, she missed the hood at times. She missed the drama. She missed the noise. The suburbs were too stiff and quiet. She never truly felt comfortable. That's why she came back Southeast and swooped up Sidra on the regular. She knew fucking with Luke was a come up though.

"And Nessa, you need to make that nigga know that even though chicks are thirsty and love a chocolate nigga with a bald head, he not gon' keep hittin' you."

Nessa damn near froze.

Silence filled the car.

"What do you mean?"

"I mean you think I can't see the bruises? Look at your damn fingers. Your fuckin' nails are gone. It looks like you were fightin' for your life. That nigga must be on some cave-man shit."

Nessa quickly looked over at her childhood friend as she shook her head. "It's not like that Sidra," she fired back. "It's too complicated. But just know he doesn't beat me."

"Oh, so that makes you a GIGANTIC punk, cause the only other explanation is that you let some bitch beat your ass."

"Sidra, forget about all that. You'll know when I'm ready for you to know. My biggest problem right now is Luke's mother. She's not making living with them easy on me," Nessa whined as she whipped a sharp curve.

"Well, just to put the shit out there, I think it's weird as hell that Luke lives with his mother anyway. I mean, I know it's a big ass house, but that's just odd. And his brother lives there too, right?"

Nessa nodded. "Yeah."

"See…somethin' ain't right about that shit."

"Yeah, when I first moved in I thought so, too. His brother doesn't bother me, he's out of the house most times, but his mother is a straight up, bitch! Every time I look around, she's eyeing me up and down all crazy and shit. She's always looking for a damn reason to fuck with me. She's got a real problem with me being with Luke. I don't know what the fuck is wrong with her."

"Fuck her. Who are you supposed to be making happy? Her or her damn son?"

"You're right. I feel you but damn."

"But damn *what*? You lookin' for her approval? Shit, if she's not tryin' to give it to you, fuck her. Luke is what matters."

"She threatened my life."

"What?"

Nessa nodded. "You heard me correctly. The bitch threatened my fucking life."

"Well, did you whoop her muthafuckin' ass?" Sidra questioned.

They both laughed.

Nessa held the side of her hip. "Please don't make me laugh. I'm so damn sore."

"So, you still not gonna tell me what happened, huh?"

"It's nothing, Sidra. Trust me."

"Well, anyway you need to kick that old ladies ass the next time she bothers you."

"You know I can't do that. I wanted to give her a quick jab to her little pointy ass face, but that's Luke's mother. I had to hold myself back."

"Fuck that shit. When a person's life is threatened, all bets are off. She thinks she can't get her head bussed wide the fuck open 'cause she's rich."

"All that *sounds* good. And of course, where you and me come from, a bitch gets dealt with for making those type of threats. But this situation is a little different."

"How is it different?"

"It just is. I have to handle it in a special kind of way."

"How?"

Don't worry. I'm going to handle it."

"How?" Sidra asked once again. She was the type of chick who rolled her neck and poked out her lips between words. "I hope you don't handle it the same way you did when you earned those war marks on your face.

"In my own way. I got it."

"Well, how did Luke feel about her threatenin' you?"

"Haven't told him yet?"

Nessa changed lanes.

"Why the fuck not?" Sidra barked and smacked her lips all at the same time. "Uggghhhh."

"Haven't spoken to him since the night it happened. That was a couple of nights ago. Haven't seen him. Haven't even heard from him. That's another thing that's got my head fucked up right now."

Nessa sped up and made the vehicle hit eighty-five after noticing two guys in a nearby Cadillac CTS trying to get her attention.

"Do you think something's wrong?"

"I don't know what to think, Sidra. My mind is fucked up right now."

"You called him?"

"Of course. Texted him, too. No answer. No response." Nessa could sense that Sidra would keep digging so she tried to end things even though she was worried as hell about Luke. The death toll in the city had been increasing by the hour so since Luke was a target, there was a strong possibility she would never see him again. "His brother said he's fine. He just needs some space."

"Space means he's fuckin' a bitch on the side. You know that, Nessa. Stop actin' like you just came off the porch. If you need me to go with you to roll up on a bitch, just let me know."

"Everything's good, Sidra. Don't worry about it."

Suddenly Nessa's phone rang. While keeping one hand on the steering wheel, she reached behind her seat into her purse and pulled out her phone. Glancing at the screen and seeing the number, she shook her head and raised her eyes back to the windshield. The number belonged to her father and she didn't want to talk to him right now. Pressing the end button and dropping the phone in her lap, his call brought back memories, memories she wasn't sure how she felt about, memories she wasn't sure if she should be leaving behind, or carrying along with her. As she drove, one in particular appeared in her mind.

Nessa had just turned nine years old. It was the day of her birthday. The sun blazed beautifully as she and her father happily made their way about the crowded circus grounds. Leading up to that day, Nessa had been practically begging her father to take her to the circus. He promised. And just like always, he kept his promise.

Mr. Byron Kingston was dressed in a short-sleeved Polo shirt, and freshly creased shorts as expensive cologne radiated from his body. He was a handsome and tall muscular man who took immense pride in his appearance. You never caught him unshaven or shabbily dressed. When he walked, he strutted. Best believe, people paid attention.

As Nessa held her dad's hand while going on rides and playing countless games, she felt so proud to be his daughter and to be by his side. It meant the world to her. He was her Superman and she always felt like his princess.

Both Nessa and her father were just coming off of the Ferris Wheel when a young man jogged up to them and whispered something in Byron's ear. Nessa couldn't hear what was whispered as she stood beside her father in a white, fluffy dress.

"You sure?" Byron asked the young man in a serious tone.

The young man nodded.

Before Nessa knew it, without a reason why, she and her father were headed back to the parking lot. Seconds later, they were in his brand new black Lincoln Town Car and leaving.

"Where are we going?" Nessa asked, barely tall enough to see over the dashboard. Her feet weren't even long enough to touch the floor.

"Gotta handle some business, sweetheart," he said. "We'll come back later."

Nessa was disappointed but didn't say anything more.

The Lincoln pulled into the parking lot of a strip club fifteen minutes later. Shutting off the engine, Byron told Nessa, "Stay in the car." He then hopped out and closed the door.

Nessa placed her knees into the seat and looked over the dashboard to see her father walk across the parking lot and approach several men. For several moments they all spoke, but Nessa couldn't make out what they were saying. Clearly though, whatever was being discussed, she could tell by the angry look on her father's face it was something that had pissed him off. Nessa continued to watch. Several moments later, her eyes widened when she saw each man, including her father, pull guns from underneath their shirts. She then watched as they headed into the strip club.

Leaning back into her seat, Nessa wondered what was going on. She wondered why her father and his men needed guns. Up until that particular moment, Nessa had never seen a gun except on television.

As time passed, one minute turned to two. Two minutes turned to several. Nessa grew impatient. But more importantly, just like any other nine year old child, she grew more and more inquisitive. She wanted to know what was going on. She had to know. So, although her father had told her to stay in the car, she got out anyway and headed across the lot. As she walked, the heels of her shoes clicked loudly. Seconds later, she reached the door, opened it and walked inside. Underneath dim lights, immediately she smelled cigarette smoke as she passed the bouncer's chair, which was empty. She also heard yelling and cursing. A short distance later, she saw a stage with a pole in the center of it. Afterward, her eyes came across a situation obviously no nine year old child should see...

Throughout the club, naked women laid sprawled out on the floor on their stomachs with their arms outstretched. Several men were also laid out. Over each of them stood the men who'd been outside conversing with her father. Their guns were pointed at each man and woman. As they were, some of the women were crying while others begged for their lives. Across the floor of the club, Nessa could hear her father's voice. There was anger in it.

Suddenly...

One of the gunmen abruptly turned to Nessa and pointed his gun at her. Caught off guard by her presence, he said, "What the fuck?"

Nessa froze in her tracks. Her eyes locked on the gun. She didn't know what to do. The other gunmen, while still keeping their guns trained on the people lying at their feet, also turned to Nessa. She was immediately scared.

"Yo, Byron!" one of the gunmen called.

Byron, with his gun pointed at the head of a man kneeling in front of him, turned around. Seeing his daughter, he said, "She's good. Come here, sweetheart."

Nessa didn't move. The entire scene scared her. She now wished she had stayed in the car like she had been told.

"It's okay, baby," Her father told her. "No one's gonna hurt you. Come here."

Nessa walked throughout the maze of pointed guns and sprawled out bodies directly to her father as fast as she could. As she did, she could see the fear and tears in each of the women's eyes. She didn't quite know what to make of it.

"Didn't I tell you to stay in the car?" Nessa's father told her when she reached him.

She nodded innocently.

Shaking his head, he said, "Well, what's done is done. We'll deal with it later."

As Nessa stood directly by her father's side, his attention went back to the man kneeling in front of him. The man was crying as he looked up at Byron with terror in his eyes.

With the gun pointed at the man's head, Byron asked his daughter, "Sweetheart, you see this man right here?"

Nessa nodded.

"He did a bad thing."

"What did he do?" she asked in a soft, delicate voice.

"He borrowed some money from me, a whole lot of money. Fifty thousand dollars to be exact. Then when it came time to pay it back, he went missing."

"Byron," the man said quickly. "I swear I wasn't hiding. I was going to get you your money. I was going..."

"Shut the fuck up!" Byron roared.

The cowering man did as he was told.

Nessa's body tensed. She'd never heard her father before.

"You borrowed that money six muthafuckin' m ago!" Byron continued. "We've been everywhere for your ass ever since. Haven't found you anywhere. The last I heard, your ass skipped town; went down to Detroit. Now, your snake ass done slithered back into town thinkin' me and my people weren't going to see you."

"Byron, I'm gonna get your money."

"Too late."

"But..."

"Shut the fuck up!"

The man dropped his head and began whimpering like a baby. He knew death was only moments away. If not death, at least something that would make him wish for death.

Speaking to his daughter again, Byron asked, "Baby, when someone does wrong, what happens?"

"They get a punishment," she answered innocently.

"Right."

The man whimpered even harder and even more loudly at the sound of those words. Sweat ran from his forehead and soaked his shirt.

"What do you think his punishment should be?" Byron asked.

"I don't know?" Nessa answered. She had no idea how to punish adults. Up until that point, she didn't even know adults received punishments.

"I think I should kill him."

"Oh God, please nooooooo," the man begged and pleaded.

"What do you think, baby?"

Nessa shook her head quickly and said, "No, daddy." Although a child, she knew what death was. She knew there was no coming back from it.

"You don't think he should die?"

"No, daddy, don't."

Byron chuckled. "The naivety of a child," he said. Then without warning...

Gun shots rang out. The gun roared loudly in Nessa's ears. Byron had squeezed the trigger. The bullet of the .45 Magnum revolver tore through the kneeling man's forehead with so much force and power it ripped his face in half. The demolition of flesh kicked back blood into Nessa's face and all over her white dress as the man's body collapsed to the floor with half his face gone and his brains splattered on the floor underneath his back.

Nessa's ears continued to ring. Her body trembled. Her eyes were on the man's dead body as blood poured from what used to be his head. It ran from his destroyed skull like water from a spilled mop bucket. The sight along with the stench radiating from the blood she was now covered with disgusted her but yet she couldn't turn her eyes away. She couldn't stop looking.

"I'm not a muthafuckin' game!" Byron yelled to everyone around him. "If you owe me, pay me!"

That was the very first time Nessa had witnessed her father kill anyone. It wasn't the last though. She personally witnessed murder and other business dealings of his numerous times throughout her childhood until the Feds finally had enough on him to destroy his enterprise. It wasn't like Nessa had her mother to run to. She'd gone missing at that time landing Nessa in the custody of Children's Services at the defenseless age of 12.

Now once again paying attention to the highway in front of her, Nessa had mixed thoughts and feelings about her father. She didn't know whether to love him or hate him. All she knew was it was him who had planted the seed in her that dictated she be a queen of these streets no matter what it took. She wanted everything he once had and then some.

Moments later, Sidra's voice brought Nessa back to reality. "You hear me, girl? Your phone is goin' off like crazy."

Nessa looked down and realized her cell was alerting her about text messages coming in. She assumed it was her father. Strangely, it wasn't.

Oh, so you ignoring me, now? Really Bitch? Really?

You think shit's a game…but I WILL kill you, too.

To read more…Filthy Rich part 1 & 2

WAIT...THERE'S MORE!

Have you always wanted to write a book?

Don't forget that we offer **FREE** publishing classes on a variety of topics throughout the year. You can sign up at TressaAzarel.com. We'll email you when free classes are being taught.

In addition, we teach our signature Publishing Boot Camp only 4 times a year! Our graduates can't stop talking about it.

WHAT IS THE BEST SELLERS PROJECT?

WATCH THE QUICK VIDEO HERE!

The Best Sellers Project (TBSP) is an online program for people who want to self-publish their books. We've assembled everything we've learned over the past 9 years in regards to publishing, publicity, distribution, traditional/ online marketing and promotion strategies into a 4-week INFORMATION INTENSE program geared towards teaching you how to **PUBLISH FOR PROFIT.**

Writing is not just a passion, but also a business that if done right, can earn you a very lucrative income.

Instead of chasing down major publishing houses, invest your money in YOURSELF and take your writing career into your own hands. There has never been a better (or easier) time than before to self-publish and we're excited to show you exactly how it's done by giving you our COMPLETE BUSINESS PLAN!

It's all about taking ACTION!

Our system works.

And this is the ONLY place where we're exposing all the self-publishing techniques we used to succeed in the literary industry.

HERE'S EXACTLY WHAT YOU'LL LEARN:

**MODULE ONE- PUBLISHING 101**

* **How to set up your publishing empire for success, even if you are a one woman/man operation, including-** how to name your company, what business structure to use in setting up your company, how to set up a business bank account, how to keep great records, how to obtain ISBNs/Barcodes/Copyrights, and how to finance your publication

* **Breaking down the elements of publishing, including-** editing, proofreading, book design, printing, and shipping and marketing

* **How to determine your ideal target audience and niche-** because your book IS NOT and SHOULD NOT be for "EVERYBODY"

* **How to pick a book cover and title that'll get your readers to be fans for life.** Because people judge books by their covers. Trust us, you don't want to have the "walk of book cover shame." And yes, that's a thing.

* How to RELAUNCH your book if you've already published, but aren't swimming in the money and raving fans like you dreamed you would (you'll thank us later)!

MODULE TWO- THE ART OF MARKETING AND PERSONAL BRANDING

* Why marketing, personal branding, and sales are soooooooo important to the success of your book…and why most books fail

* How to build a POWERFUL personal brand

* How to create an EFFECTIVE marketing campaign that'll practically have your books selling themselves. You'll also receive a sample 30-day marketing plan from Tiphani's very own bestselling series.

* How to release the FEAR of promoting the book you've worked so hard to launch. This is a serious topic that's stopping you (women especially) from making serious money. We're on a mission to end the SHAME around promotion and sales, once and for all.

* How to MASTER the art of selling– because if you want to make any money, you're going to want to know this.

* Fearless Self-Promotion Strategies

MODULE THREE- DISTRIBUTION AND PRINTING

* How to obtain **MAJOR** distribution and placement in **MAJOR** chain and online bookstores **BEFORE** your book comes out

* How to sell your books to non-traditional markets- because you never want to put your eggs all in one basket

* The difference between book printers and commercial printers and which one will give you the most bang for your buck

* How to negotiate your printing costs...like a **BOSS!**

* How many books to print for your initial run and how to price them

MODULE FOUR- PROFIT!!!!!!!

* How to create a book budget to avoid going broke (Yup, we're breaking down alllllllll your costs)

* How to finance your own publication- these days, it's never been easier

* How much money you can **REALLY** make in the publishing industry

* What parts of the year affect your sales for better and for worse?

* How to be just as good as the major publishing houses- we'll teach you how to reinvest your money back into

your business to make more money, how to get licensing deals, and how to get nationally recognized.

After implementing what Azarel + Tiphani taught me, I was able to write a book about my life story and build a huge buzz for my book that skyrocketed it to #1 on Amazon…all from pre-order sales! The knowledge that they so generously give is priceless!

~Winter Ramos, Reality TV Star + Author of *Game Over*

Now, Here's That Amazing, Super Exclusive Bonus We Mentioned Earlier:

Be one of the next 30 people who sign up right now for, **The Best Sellers Project** and receive access to **"Your Next Chapter (YNC),"** a private group strategy session with Azarel and I which includes an audit of your book (or book idea if you're just getting started).

We've limited **YNC** to an intimate group of 30 because in addition to your book audit, we're also giving you valuable marketing and promotional ideas for your specific project. This, my sweet friend, is an AMAZING offer!! *(A $997 value, FREE for the next 30 people who sign up)*

Azarel and I are thrilled to help you make your writing and publishing dreams a reality.

But Wait, There's More:

231

You'll also receive our interactive workbook that's jam packed with:

* Everything from ultra-positive thinking techniques to sample marketing plans from our most successful projects and visionary goal-setting. **Useful. Simple.** *Potent.*

* **Our personal resource Rolodex** of editors, book cover designers, web/graphic designers, printers, copywriters and more.

*Winning strategies, tools and mantras to help you stay motivated. **For life.**

(A $297 Value!)

Note: The Best Sellers Project interactive workbook isn't a self-help workbook, a bundle of empty encouragement, or formulaic tip sheet. **It's a proven system of thought-shifting techniques for people who are serious about taking their writing and self-publishing career to the next level.**

Fortunately, we know you're serious. Or you wouldn't be here.

The Best Sellers Project taught me more in 30 days than a marketing class I took in college taught me in an entire semester!"

~Crystal G. Edwards, Queens, NY

You Have Questions…We Got Answers!
How much does TBSP cost and what's included?

232

* 4 high powered mentoring sessions with Tiphani and Azarel, which includes our most powerful ideas, advice, and resources (a $2,500 value)

* Super exclusive "**Your Next Chapter**" bonus offer that's only available to the first 30 people who sign up (a $1,500 value)

* Custom workbook. Useful. Simple. Potent. (a $297 value)

That's over $4,000 of Value.

You pay $497!

Do you offer payment plans?

Yes! Email us to inquire about our payment plans- Tiphani@tiphanimontgomery.com

Where is the class located?

Online.

What are the dates and times?

The live group strategy and mentoring sessions will be held on:

Wednesday, September 2nd at 9pm EST

Wednesday, September 9th at 9pm EST

Wednesday, September 16th at 9pm EST

Wednesday, September 23rd at 9pm EST

What if I can't make the live strategy sessions? Will they be recorded?

Absolutely. Everything will be recorded and delivered to your inbox as soon as class is over.

Who is The Best Sellers Project for?

TBSP is for authors and entrepreneurs who want to learn how to build a platform and successfully publish your own print and eBooks!

Whether it's your personal life story you want turned into a memoir, a self-help book to help guide others through difficult journeys in life, or that best-selling novel that's been stuck in your soul for years, this boot camp is for you!

If my ultimate goal is to be published by a major publisher, do I still need to take this program?

Yes and no.

No, if you have found a literary agent and you have publishers ready to buy your book. In that case, you need to write a book proposal.

Yes, if you can't find an agent or a publisher to touch you (or your book) with a ten foot pole and you're ready to take matters into your own hands.

The truth is, a publishing house isn't likely to give you a book deal if you don't have a platform already established. A platform is an audience of fans or followers that you've built a relationship with and will buy what you're selling. A major publisher wants answers to questions like how many Facebook, Twitter, Instagram and YouTube followers do you have? How many people do you have on your email list? How much work have you done to market yourself before coming to them?

It's a common misconception that it's the publisher's responsibility to market your book. It's not. This responsibility relies solely on you and unless you've conquered this giant, your chances of getting an agent or a book deal as a first time author is slim to none.

The publishing industry is changing. Authors have a chance to make their own rules, which was an option that wasn't available to you before.

Remember, **50 Shades a Grey** was rejected by every publisher she proposed her book to. She went on to self-publish her project as an eBook and, well, you know the rest (hint: it involves lots of these——> $$$$$).

In **TBSP** we're going to teach you how to build a platform and market your book to the right audience.

How can I reach you if I have more questions?

Email: lcbinfo2013@gmail.com and I'll get right back to ya!

Because of the information I learned in The Best Sellers Project, I was able to produce a rock solid social media and marketing campaign creating serious buzz before my book was even out and a referral to a web designer who made me a beautifully website. After the class my first novel, *Where Did We Go Wrong?*, hit three best sellers list including #1 (with 150+ five star reviews) on Amazon!

The Best Sellers Project gave me all the tools, secrets, and strategies I needed to become a BEST SELLER!"

~Monica Mathis-Stowe, Best Selling Author of **_Where Did We Go Wrong?_**

After participating in **The Best Sellers Project** I am crystal clear on how to get my message out to the world in a way that is unique to me and speaks to those people who my books are created for. The Q&A sessions and resource guides are priceless and have helped me save major time and money publishing my book. My confidence has skyrocketed because I now have all the

tools, resources and strategies to impact more lives and make more money doing what I love- Helping Others Transform! Thank you!

~Angel Richards, CEO of Angel Richards Publishing, Inc., Tampa, FL

Briana Nicole

Debut novel

Heart Breaker

AVAILABLE NOW!

P. Sharee's

Debut novel

Fit for a King

AVAILABLE NOW!

Pre-Order

Miss KP's

A Wife's Betrayal

COMING SOON!

Pre-Order

D. Henderson's

Career Criminal: The First of a Trilogy

COMING SOON!

Pre-Order

Carlton Brown's

Debut Novel

2 Sides of a Penny

COMING SOON

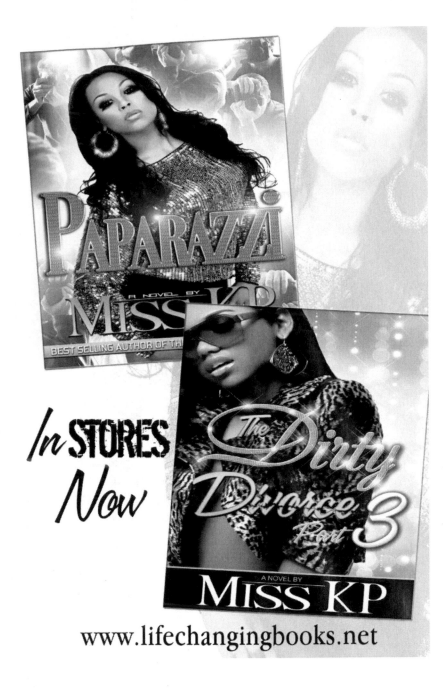

In STORES Now

www.lifechangingbooks.net

CHECK OUT THESE TITLES
BY: *Kendall Banks*

LCB BOOK TITLES

See More Titles At
www.lifechangingbooks.net

CHECK OUT THESE LCB SEQUELS

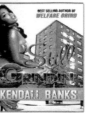

245

ORDER FORM

MAIL TO:
PO Box 423
Brandywine, MD 20613
301-362-6508

| Date: | Phone: |
| Email: | |

| Ship to: |
| Address: |
| City & State: | Zip: |

Make all money orders and cashiers checks payable to: **Life Changing Books**

Qty.	ISBN	Title	Release Date	Price
	0-9741394-2-4	Bruised by Azarel	Jul-05	$ 15.00
	0-9741394-7-5	Bruised 2: The Ultimate Revenge by Azarel	Oct-06	$ 15.00
	0-9741394-3-2	Secrets of a Housewife by J. Tremble	Feb-06	$ 15.00
	0-9741394-6-7	The Millionaire Mistress by Tiphani	Nov-06	$ 15.00
	1-934230-99-5	More Secrets More Lies by J. Tremble	Feb-07	$ 15.00
	1-934230-95-2	A Private Affair by Mike Warren	May-07	$ 15.00
	1-934230-96-0	Flexin & Sexin Volume 1	Jun-07	$ 15.00
	1-934230-89-8	Still a Mistress by Tiphani	Nov-07	$ 15.00
	1-934230-91-X	Daddy's House by Azarel	Nov-07	$ 15.00
	1-934230-88-X	Naughty Little Angel by J. Tremble	Feb-08	$ 15.00
	1-934230820	Rich Girls by Kendall Banks	Oct-08	$ 15.00
	1-934230839	Expensive Taste by Tiphani	Nov-08	$ 15.00
	1-934230782	Brooklyn Brothel by C. Stecko	Jan-09	$ 15.00
	1-934230669	Good Girl Gone bad by Danette Majette	Mar-09	$ 15.00
	1-934230804	From Hood to Hollywood by Sasha Raye	Mar-09	$ 15.00
	1-934230707	Sweet Swagger by Mike Warren	Jun-09	$ 15.00
	1-934230677	Carbon Copy by Azarel	Jul-09	$ 15.00
	1-934230723	Millionaire Mistress 3 by Tiphani	Nov-09	$ 15.00
	1-934230715	A Woman Scorned by Ericka Williams	Nov-09	$ 15.00
	1-934230685	My Man Her Son by J. Tremble	Feb-10	$ 15.00
	1-924230731	Love Heist by Jackie D.	Mar-10	$ 15.00
	1-934230812	Flexin & Sexin Volume 2	Apr-10	$ 15.00
	1-934230748	The Dirty Divorce by Miss KP	May-10	$ 15.00
	1-934230758	Chedda Boyz by CJ Hudson	Jul-10	$ 15.00
	1-934230766	Snitch by VegasClarke	Oct-10	$ 15.00
	1-934230693	Money Maker by Tonya Ridley	Oct-10	$ 15.00
	1-934230774	The Dirty Divorce Part 2 by Miss KP	Nov-10	$ 15.00
	1-934230170	The Available Wife by Carla Pennington	Jan-11	$ 15.00
	1-934230774	One Night Stand by Kendall Banks	Feb-11	$ 15.00
	1-934230278	Bitter by Danette Majette	Feb-11	$ 15.00
	1-934230299	Married to a Balla by Jackie D.	May-11	$ 15.00
	1-934230308	The Dirty Divorce Part 3 by Miss KP	Jun-11	$ 15.00
	1-934230316	Next Door Nympho By CJ Hudson	Jun-11	$ 15.00
	1-934230286	Bedroom Gangsta by J. Tremble	Sep-11	$ 15.00
	1-934230340	Another One Night Stand by Kendall Banks	Oct-11	$ 15.00
	1-934230359	The Available Wife Part 2 by Carla Pennington	Nov-11	$ 15.00
	1-934230332	Wealthy & Wicked by Chris Renee	Jan-12	$ 15.00
	1-934230375	Life After a Balla by Jackie D.	Mar-12	$ 15.00
	1-934230251	V.I.P. by Azarel	Apr-12	$ 15.00
	1-934230383	Welfare Grind by Kendall Banks	May-12	$ 15.00
	1-934230413	Still Grindin' by Kendall Banks	Sep-12	$ 15.00
	1-934230391	Paparazzi by Miss KP	Oct-13	$ 15.00
	1-93423043X	Cashin' Out by Jai Nicole	Nov-12	$ 15.00
	1-934230634	Welfare Grind Part 3 by Kendall Banks	Mar-13	$ 15.00
	1-934230642	Game Over by Winter Ramos	Apr-13	$15.99
			Total for Books	$

| * Prison Orders- Please allow up to three (3) weeks for delivery. | **Shipping Charges** (add $4.95 for 1-4 books*) | $ |
| | **Total Enclosed** (add lines) | $ |

Please Note: We are not held responsible for returned prison orders. Make sure the facility will receive books before ordering.

*Shipping and Handling of 5-10 books is $6.95, please contact us if your order is more than 10 books. (301)362-6508

246